The Hardy Boys®
in
The Ghost at Skeleton Rock

Hardy Boys® Mystery Stories in Armada

For contractual reasons, Armada has been obliged to publish from No. 57 onwards before publishing Nos. 41–56. These missing numbers will be published as soon as possible.

The Hardy Boys® Mystery Stories

The Ghost at Skeleton Rock

Franklin W. Dixon

Armada

First published in the U.K. in 1974 by
William Collins Sons & Co. Ltd, London and Glasgow
First published in Armada in 1984
This impression 1987

Armada is an imprint of
the Children's Division, part of
the Collins Publishing Group,
8 Grafton Street, London W1X 3LA

Printed in Great Britain by.
William Collins Sons & Co. Ltd, Glasgow

CONTENTS

The huge man swept Joe aside with a single blow of his great arm.

·1·

A Puzzling Message

"LET's see if you can get us down in one piece, Frank!" Blond, seventeen-year-old Joe Hardy leaned forward in the aeroplane as his brother circled in for a landing at the Bayport airfield.

"Don't worry, Joe. If we crack up the first time, I'll try again," the dark-haired boy quipped. Frank, who was a year older than Joe, grinned as he eased the craft downwards in a graceful turn.

A third occupant of the plane, the usual pilot, smiled and said, "You're doing fine, Frank." Jack Wayne, lean-faced and tanned, was Mr Hardy's pilot on all his chartered flights. Today Jack was teaching the boys how to fly the new six-seater, single-engine plane which their father had purchased recently.

"There's a gusty wind, so come in at a slightly higher airspeed," Jack reminded his pupil.

Frank's pulse quickened as he lined up on the runway and reduced power. The beautiful blue-and-white craft descended in a normal glide.

The landing strip and parked planes below seemed to rush up at them, the details growing larger as Frank headed towards the ground.

"Watch out for those telephone lines!" Joe cried out.

The wires loomed squarely in front of the plane's nose. If Frank had judged his glide angle correctly, the wires should be dropping below his field of vision. Instead, they seemed to be coming straight at the plane!

Frank gulped with panic. *Would they crash?* Trying hard to keep cool, he eased back on the controls. With barely a split second to go, the ship nosed upwards and cleared the wires!

Moments later, the plane's wheels touched down in a perfect landing and the craft rolled to a stop. Frank climbed out after the others, feeling a bit weak.

"Quick thinking, boy!" Joe slapped his brother on the back. "Only next time, please don't shave it so close!"

Frank heaved a sigh. "I didn't think—I just acted! How come you didn't take over, Jack?"

"I figured you'd do the right thing"—the pilot chuckled—"and you did!" Suddenly his face clouded and he snapped his fingers. "I clean forgot to tell you!"

"What?" the boys chorused.

"A message your father gave me just before I took off from San Juan." Early that morning Jack had returned after flying Mr Hardy to Puerto Rico the previous day on a top-secret case. "Sorry. Giving flying lessons must make me absent-minded." He handed the boys a piece of paper.

" 'Find Hugo purple turban', " Frank and Joe read aloud. They stared at the paper, completely baffled by the cryptic message.

Jack went on to explain that Mr Hardy had quickly jotted down the strange words, then handed the paper to him. "He did say," Jack added, "that he couldn't give any more details right then. He'd spotted a man he wanted to shadow."

The boys racked their brains for a moment in silence. Neither could think of anyone in Bayport named Hugo.

"Oh, well," Frank said, smiling, "we'll try to figure it out later. Thanks for the flying lesson, Jack."

After arranging for their next flight, the boys went to the car park, where they had left their convertible.

"I'll drive," said Frank. In a few minutes the boys were heading towards their pleasant, tree-shaded home at the corner of Elm and High streets.

The dazzling June sun shone down on them as they talked over the odd message.

"We'll have to twirl our brains for this one," Joe commented as they pulled into the Hardys' gravel drive. "I wonder who Hugo is. Someone in Bayport, maybe?"

"Let's try the phone book," Frank suggested. "Hugo could be someone's last name."

As the boys strode in through the kitchen door, their mother was trimming the crust on an apple pie. Each son gave her a quick kiss on the cheek, then Frank said, "We're trying to figure out a code message from Dad. Have you any idea who 'Hugo purple turban' might be?"

Mrs Hardy, slim and pretty, shook her head as she slid the pie into the oven. "Not the faintest, but it sounds like the start of another interesting case."

Her husband, Fenton Hardy, had been a crack detective for years in the New York City Police Department. Later, when he retired and moved to the coastal town of Bayport, Mr Hardy had become internationally famous as a private investigator. His two sons had skilfully assisted him on many of his cases.

Frank, intrigued by his father's newest assignment, hurried to the telephone book with Joe at his heels, and leafed through the pages of names beginning with H.

"Let's see now." Frank moistened his finger. "Hugo . . . Hugo . . . Here we are! Just three of them," he added after a moment. "It should be simple to find the right man."

Joe dialled the first number. The quavering, high-pitched voice of an elderly woman answered the phone. In reply to Joe's question, she snapped suspiciously, "A purple turban? What on earth are you talking about?"

Joe tried to explain. But the woman's reaction was unfriendly, as if she suspected some kind of a hoax.

"Young man, I can't make head nor tail of what you're saying. Sounds to me as if you're trying to be funny—or else you've got the wrong number!"

With a loud sniff, she hung up.

"Whew! Guess I didn't do too well on that one," Joe told his brother. "Next time remind me not to sound like such a crackpot!"

Joe dialled another number. The listing on this one was·"Hugo's Meat Market."

"*Yah*, I'm Hugo," said a voice in a heavy German accent.

Joe explained that he was doing some private detective work and was trying to locate a person named Hugo who had some connection with a purple turban or maybe someone known as "Hugo Purple Turban."

"*Ach*, no, I never hear of anyone like that," the

butcher replied. "But if you like some good liverwurst, just drop in here at any time!"

Frank chuckled as Joe hung up the phone. "We're getting nowhere fast. Let me try."

The third Hugo listed was a Wilfred K., a jeweller and watch-repair expert.

" 'Hugo purple turban?' Hmm," the man responded thoughtfully. "Sounds to me as if it might refer to that fortune teller."

"Fortune teller?"

"The Great Hugo, he calls himself—at least that's the name painted on his trailer. He has a tent pitched beside the road, on Route 10, just north of town."

"Thanks a lot, sir!" Frank exclaimed, with a surge of excitement. "Sounds like a swell lead!"

As he put down the phone, a peppery feminine voice spoke up from behind the boys. "Before you get too deep in another mystery, take my advice and—"

"Oh, hi, Aunt Gertrude!" Joe smiled and turned round.

Frank said mischievously, "Aunt Gertrude's just jealous, Joe, because she doesn't know all the facts!"

"Nonsense!" retorted their aunt, a tall, angular woman, who was Mr Hardy's maiden sister.

Although Aunt Gertrude would never admit it, Frank and Joe knew that she was just as deeply intrigued by the Hardys' cases as the boys and their father.

Frank told her about Mr Hardy's puzzling communication "Hugo purple turban" and went on, "The man I just talked to on the phone seemed to think it might refer to some fortune teller called The Great Hugo."

"The Great Hugo! Why, of course!" Aunt Gertrude's eyes narrowed with a look of suspicion.

"Do you know him?" Joe asked eagerly.

"I've heard about him—and what I've heard isn't good!" Miss Hardy explained that two women she knew had gone to have The Great Hugo tell their fortunes. After leaving his tent, they had discovered money missing from their handbags, which they had hung on the backs of their chairs.

"You mean Hugo stole it?" Frank asked.

"Who else? Naturally, the women couldn't *prove* it," Miss Hardy added, pursing her lips, "but there's no doubt in their minds."

The two boys exchanged glances. "He could be the man we're looking for," Frank remarked.

Joe nodded. "Let's check with Chief Collig."

As head of the Bayport Police Department, Chief Collig had co-operated with the Hardys on many of their cases. When Frank telephoned him, the chief said that he was acquainted with The Great Hugo and had had complaints about him.

"He's as phony as a nine-dollar bill, but so far we haven't enough evidence to take him in."

Frank thanked the chief, hung up, and passed the information to his brother.

"Come on! Let's go have a look at Hugo!" Joe urged.

Frank reversed the car out of the drive and headed for Route 10. North of town, they sighted a bright, orange-coloured tent just off the road.

Near the tent stood a house trailer of the same orange colour. It was hitched to a somewhat battered bu very powerful-looking black car of an expensive make.

"There it is," Frank murmured, slowing down. The tent bore a sign reading:

THE GREAT HUGO
WORLD-FAMOUS MYSTIC
Private Readings by Appointment

Frank parked the convertible under a tree and the boys walked towards the tent. As they were about to enter, a man, at least six and a half feet tall, and with an extremely large head, loomed up in front of them, barring the way.

His swarthy, hook-nosed face gave the man a menacing air. But what jolted both boys were his clothes. He wore baggy trousers, Oriental slippers with pointed, curled-up toes, and a purple turban!

"What is it you wish?" he demanded in a deep, harsh voice.

"We came to have our fortunes told," Joe said evenly.

"I do not tell fortunes—I am only Abdul, a helper," the man grunted. "You wait outside. I go see if The Great Hugo will receive you."

Abdul entered the tent, dropping the flap across the entrance. Tense with excitement, the young detectives waited, but not for long. A moment later Abdul reappeared.

"I bring good news! The Great Hugo will see you at once!" he announced.

He drew aside the tent flap, bowed low, and invited the boys to enter. Cautiously they stepped into the gloomy interior. The walls of the tent were hung with dark draperies. Only the pale glow of a shaded lamp suffused the gloom. Soft rugs lay underfoot.

At a table covered with a silver-fringed black velvet cloth sat a slim, short man with a pointed brown beard. Before him on the table lay a crystal ball.

"So—you have come to have your fortunes told," he murmured. "Please be seated."

As the boys sank down on to two leather hassocks, Hugo's queer yellowish eyes seemed to be sizing them up shrewdly.

Stalling for time in order to observe the place carefully, Frank said, "Before you start, sir, perhaps you'd better tell us how much it's going to cost."

The Great Hugo waved his hand carelessly. "My usual fee is five dollars. But since I am not busy today I will take you both for two dollars."

The boys reached for their wallets and produced one dollar apiece. Hugo whisked the money out of sight, then concentrated his gaze on the crystal ball. In a few moments he seemed to go into a trance.

"I see an aeroplane—a trip over water," the fortune teller said in a droning voice. "The scene in the crystal ball is changing. . . . I see trouble! Danger!"

Suddenly Frank felt a hand groping into his pocket. Gripping the thief's wrist, he whirled round. It was Abdul!

"Oh, no, you don't!" Frank exclaimed, jumping up and forcing the man backwards. But with lightning speed the brawny fellow stunned him with a blow on the chin. Frank staggered groggily.

Joe leaped to his brother's aid. But he was quickly grabbed by Abdul. As Joe struggled to get away from the giant, he knocked over the table and the crystal ball.

At one end of the tent Hugo the Mystic was shouting commands to Abdul, and edging towards a position behind the three. A moment later black hoods were thrown over the boys' heads.

"Let's get rid of them, Abdul, and leave—quick!" Hugo growled.

· 2 ·

The Suspicious Trailer

THEIR heads covered, Frank and Joe were hurled to
the ground. Resistance was futile. Quickly their hands
and feet were bound. Then they were dragged out of
the tent and into some bushes. Footsteps indicated that
their attackers had left.

"Joe! Joe, can you hear me?" Frank shouted. The
hood muffled his voice, but he was able to make out
Joe's response.

"Right here, Frank."

From a short distance away came confused sounds
as if the tent were being quickly taken down and
stowed in the trailer. Soon the engine of a car roared to
life and the vehicle went rumbling off down the busy
main road.

Meanwhile, the boys twisted and turned in a frantic
effort to loosen their bonds. This was not the only time
they had found themselves in a predicament like this
one.

Ever since their first big case, *The Mystery of the Aztec
Warrior*, the brothers had often been in tight spots. But
always their quick, cool thinking had enabled them to
outwit their adversaries. In their most recent case, they

18

had undertaken a hazardous trip to the Northwest Territories to solve *The Viking Symbol Mystery*.

By the time Frank got his hands free, his wrists were rubbed nearly raw. He jerked the black hood off his head and saw Joe still straining to free himself.

"Here! I'll do it!" Frank offered.

Quickly he removed his brother's hood. In a few moments both were free and on their feet.

Joe peered at the tyre tracks of the vanished car and trailer. "They made a neat getaway," he said bitterly.

"Which means The Great Hugo must have been the Hugo we want!" Frank said grimly.

"Then what are we waiting for?" Joe sprinted towards the convertible. "Let's go after him!"

Before leaving, Frank insisted that they examine the tyre tracks of both the vanished car and the trailer. Then the boys ran to their convertible. Frank took the wheel and they left in a spurt of sand and gravel. Luckily, Route 10 ran straight north for almost twelve miles before intersecting another major thoroughfare.

En route there were several dirt-road turnoffs. Frank and Joe stopped at each one and got out to inspect all tyre marks on them. But they found no sign of the vehicles belonging to Hugo and Abdul.

"Probably they're heading out of the state," Joe remarked.

"Wait a minute. Let's try this caravan site up ahead," Frank suggested. It was situated less than half a mile from the road intersection.

He braked the car and swung over on to the shoulder of the road. Again the boys climbed out.

"It's a hundred-to-one shot," Frank admitted, "but Hugo might have turned in here to throw us off the trail."

"He'll have a tough time hiding that orange trailer," Joe said. "Say look!" He broke off with a gasp and grabbed Frank's arm. "Over there!"

Frank turned to face the direction in which his brother was staring. An orange trailer!

Though partly hidden from view by other vehicles, the trailer looked like the one used by Hugo and Abdul. The boys approached it casually, trying not to attract any attention.

Their hopes, however, were soon dashed. Frilly lace curtains showed in the windows of the trailer. In front of it a fat, baldheaded man in Bermuda shorts lounged in a deck chair. A moment later a woman came out carrying a baby.

Frank smiled to hide his disappointment. "Okay. So our long shot didn't pay off."

"Now what?"

Frank considered. "Once Hugo hits the crossroads there's no telling which way he'll head. Guess we'd better notify the police."

Across the road from the caravan site was a roadside shop with a petrol pump. The boys hurried over and put through a call to Chief Collig from the phone box outside.

"I'll send out a radio alert," the officer promised after hearing Frank's story. "Maybe the highway patrol can pick those men up before they cross the state line."

"Thanks, Chief! We'll keep in touch," said Frank.

Somewhat dejectedly, the boys plodded back to their

convertible. "What a wild-goose chase!" Frank groaned.

On the way back to Bayport, Joe brightened suddenly as a thought struck him. "Maybe we could spot Hugo's trailer from the air. That bright-orange trailer ought to stand out on any road!"

Frank agreed. "We can ask Jack Wayne to take us up," he said.

When they reached home, Frank parked the convertible in the drive and the boys hurried into the house. Before they were halfway through the kitchen, the telephone rang.

"Maybe it's Chief Collig with some news!" Joe exclaimed. He reached the hall first and scooped up the phone. "Hello."

"This is Chet, Joe," came a breathless voice over the line. "Something's up! I need help right away—over at my place."

Chet Morton, a chubby pal of the Hardys, attended Bayport High with them. Good-natured and fond of eating, he was usually slow moving and easy going. But now his voice throbbed with fearful urgency.

"Chet! What's this all about?" Joe demanded.

"I can't explain over the phone, but get here fast," his friend pleaded. "This is important!"

"Okay. We'll be there pronto."

"What's wrong?" Frank asked as Joe hung up.

"Search me. Chet seems to be all worked up. Sounds as if he's in real trouble. He wants us to come out to the farm on the double."

"All right. But first let me call Jack Wayne."

Snatching up the phone, Frank dialled Jack's cubby-hole office at the airport. When the pilot answered,

Frank gave him a quick account of their adventure with Hugo and Abdul. Jack was thunderstruck to learn that the brothers were already on the trail of "Hugo purple turban."

"Joe and I figure," Frank went on, "that the quickest way to spot the trailer is from the air. Could you go up and reconnoitre a bit?"

"Sure," Jack replied.

Frank described the black car and orange trailer, then hung up and hurried out to the car with Joe. Twenty minutes later they reached the Morton farmhouse on the outskirts of Bayport.

The boys ran up to the front door and rang the bell. Two pretty girls answered the door. One was Chet's dark-haired sister, Iola. The other, a blonde with sparkling brown eyes, was her chum, Callie Shaw. The two girls often double-dated Frank and Joe.

"Well! Imagine meeting you two here!" said Iola in pleased surprise.

"You're just in time," Callie said. She held up a puppet dressed like Little Red Riding Hood. "We were just practising for a puppet show we're going to give at the hospital bazaar. You two can help us—"

"Where's Chet?" Joe interrupted.

"Why, out in the barn," said Iola. "But—"

"Come on, Frank!"

Without waiting to explain, Frank and Joe rushed outside and ran round the side of the barn to the back. Voices became more audible at every step. Suddenly both boys pulled up short and stared at each other in amazement.

"Did you hear somebody mention the name Hugo?" Joe whispered breathlessly.

Freezing in their tracks, the Hardys listened intently.

"We'll get the Hardys and get 'em good, Hugo!" said a rough voice.

"Yeah," came the chuckling reply. "We'll ambush them tonight!"

·3·

The Hijacked Dummy

"AMBUSH?" Joe flashed his brother a startled glance.

Frank clenched his fists. "I don't know what's going on back there, but let's find out!"

With their hearts thumping and their fists ready for trouble, the Hardys dashed round the corner of the barn, then stopped dead in open-mouthed astonishment. The only person in sight was Chet Morton, propped up against the back of the barn.

"Hi, fellows!" he greeted them, lifting his eyebrows in an innocent, deadpan look. "Expecting someone else?"

"But where are those two men we heard?" Joe asked in surprise.

"You're looking at 'em, pal. Both of 'em!" Chet replied.

To prove this, he switched over to his two "tough guy" voices and uttered a few more blood-curdling threats.

"*You?*" Frank could hardly believe his ears.

"That's right." The stout boy chuckled. "A slight case of ventriloquism, gentlemen. Learned it from books. Thought it might come in handy helping you fellows on your cases." He burst into laughter. "Oh, boy, did you two ever fall for my act—hook, line, and sinker!"

"And that phone call begging for help?" Joe growled. "That was just a trick, too, to get us over here?"

Chet nodded. "But don't hold it against me."

The Hardy boys grinned, then Frank said, "You sure fooled us. I'll say you're good."

"I sure am!" Chet agreed. "In fact, I may make a career out of ventriloquism," he went on, turning serious. "Man, I can see myself now, doing a big show on television! Chet Morton, Man of Many Voices—World's Greatest Imitator!"

This time it was the Hardys' chance to needle their friend. "World's Greatest Appetite, you mean!" Joe hooted. "Otherwise known as Chet Morton, Man of Many Helpings!"

Chet's moonface took on a hurt look. "Okay, okay. Just because I happen to appreciate good food," he sulked. "If you fellows don't think I'm ready for the big time, just listen to this."

He jerked his thumb towards the house and whispered, "Here comes my pesky cousin, Jinny."

A moment later a little girl's shrill, whiny voice seemed to come drifting round the corner of the barn:

"Oh, Chet! Your mother says you better get in the house right this minute and start cleaning up the basement! Y'hear me? You better come quick, or I'm gonna tell her just where you're hiding!"

The boys were amazed at the demonstration. Chet's lips had hardly moved.

"That's pretty convincing, Chet," said Frank.

Chet looked somewhat mollified. "It ought to be good," he bragged. "I've been studying and practising secretly for a whole month. I'm even thinking of buying a Hugo!"

"A Hugo?" Frank and Joe gasped together.

"Sure," Chet said calmly. "The same kind of dummy Professor Fox uses."

"Oh!" The Hardys relaxed as they recalled the act to which Chet was referring. Professor Fox was a star ventriloquist on TV. His dummy, Hugo, had become so popular that it was being copied and sold on a large scale. The dummy came in various-priced models.

"I'm going to get the most expensive Hugo on the market," Chet bragged. "I've been saving to buy it by doing extra chores around the farm. I have enough money now."

Just then Chet's bull terrier, Spud, came wandering out to see what was going on.

"Watch me fool him," Chet said with a wink at his friends. "Over there, boy!"

He pointed to a clump of bushes and threw his voice once again:

"*Here, Spud! Come on, boy! Got a nice thick juicy steak for you! Come on, fella!*"

Instead of responding, the bull terrier stood still, eyeing his master quizzically.

Chet lost his temper. "Well, go on, dopey. What're you waiting for?" The bull terrier merely panted and wagged his tail.

"Wow! Did you ever fool him!" Frank gibed. Both he and Joe doubled up with laughter.

Chet turned beet red and grumpily threw his dog a

stick to chase. Then he casually suggested, "Let's get some lemonade and cookies."

On the way back to the house, Joe said thoughtfully, "Some of those Hugos come with Oriental turbans, don't they, Chet?"

"The better models do," replied the stout boy. "Why?"

"Oh, just a hunch I had about something." Turning to his brother, Joe went on, "Do you suppose Dad's message might have referred to one of those dummies?"

Frank nodded. "It's an idea."

"Don't tell me you fellows are wrestling with another mystery?" Chet inquired uneasily.

"Right. And you're just the one to help us solve it," Joe told Chet, slapping him on the back.

"Not me!" Chet protested with a shudder.

Getting involved in the Hardys' crime cases always gave Chet the jitters, although the roly-poly high-school boy had already been through several dangerous adventures with Joe and Frank.

"This won't get you into any danger," Joe assured him. Hastily he explained about the puzzling message which Mr Hardy had sent from Puerto Rico.

"Where do I come in?" Chet asked suspiciously.

"When you go shopping for a Hugo dummy, just keep your eyes open. Better still, let us go with you. Maybe we'll run across some kind of a clue."

"We-e-ell . . . I guess I can go along that far with you," Chet agreed grudgingly.

"Where did you plan on buying your dummy?" Frank asked.

"Bivven's Novelty Shop. That's where I've been getting all my books on ventriloquism."

"Okay. Let's go!"

After stopping in the house for lemonade with the girls and to pick up Chet's wallet, the three boys piled into the convertible and drove off. A few minutes later they stopped in front of the novelty shop on King Street.

A bell tinkled as they walked in and Mr Bivven, the squat, baldheaded proprietor, came out of the back room to greet them.

He beamed at the trio across the counter. "Something you'd like, boys?"

Chet said he wanted to look over the store's stock of ventriloquist's dummies.

One by one, Mr Bivven showed his stock, but Chet turned them all down and asked for a Hugo dummy. The proprietor went to his storeroom and emerged presently with a cardboard box. It contained a Hugo dummy, clad in a tuxedo and red turban.

"I just received this today," Mr Bivven said. Taking out the dummy, Chet set it on the counter and began putting on an impromptu ventriloquist act.

Frank watched, chuckling, for a moment. Then he picked up the instruction sheet which was lying in the box and began to read it. The simple directions were printed in three languages—English, French, and Spanish.

The doorbell tinkled again and two men entered the shop. One was tall and rough-looking, with large ears that stuck out from his head; the other was short and swarthy-complexioned.

Joe, who was standing alongside Chet and Frank, watched the men out of the corner of his eye. They stopped in front of a trayful of water pistols and began looking through them. It looked as though they were killing time until the proprietor could serve them.

"Okay. I guess I'll take this one," Chet decided finally.

As he pulled out his wallet to pay for the dummy, Mr Bivven put the figure back in the box and started to wrap it.

"Good thing you stopped in today, son," he remarked chattily. "This here's the only Hugo in stock. If you'd waited any longer, I reckon you'd have been plumb out o' luck."

"Just a minute!" said the tall man, stepping forward. "That dummy is exactly what I been lookin' for. How much is the kid payin' for it?"

"Twenty-eight dollars and ninety-five cents."

"Then I'll give you thirty-five bucks!"

Mr Bivven hesitated. He hated to lose the extra profit, but Chet was a good customer and he didn't want to offend him.

"Nope. I'm sorry, the deal's already closed."

"Forty-five!"

Mr Bivven gulped and shook his head. "I told you before, mister, it's no go. First come, first served. Dummy's already sold to Chet here."

Grinning triumphantly, Chet counted out the money. But as the proprietor turned to ring up the sale on the cash register, the short man suddenly whipped out a shiny, blue-steel revolver.

"It's a cinch *that* gun's no toy!" thought Joe, wincing.

"We want that dummy!" snarled the short man.

As Chet stood quaking, the tall fellow grabbed Hugo off the counter!

· 4 ·

A Double Burglary

THE armed intruders kept the boys and Mr Bivven covered as they backed hastily towards the door with the Hugo dummy.

"Don't try any hero stuff and don't call the cops after we leave," warned the swarthy gunman. "If you do, you'll sure regret it!"

Then the tall man jerked open the door and the two dashed out to a car parked at the kerb. Frank and Joe rushed to the window just in time to see the short man slide behind the wheel.

"Watch it, fellows," Chet begged.

Pale and trembling with excitement, he half expected to see the store's show window shattered by a hail of bullets. Instead, the engine roared and the car, a green saloon, sped away.

"No luck on the licence number!" Joe groaned. "The rear plate was caked with mud."

"After them!" Frank cried, dashing out.

The Hardys leaped into their convertible and took off. Luckily, traffic was light. In the distance Joe caught a glimpse of the getaway car. "There it is!" he yelled.

Frank speeded up. The green car whined in a turn to the right at the next intersection. As the convertible followed, the other car suddenly put on a fresh burst of speed.

"They must have spotted us in their rear-view mirror," Frank muttered through clenched teeth.

As the chase continued, the green car shot through a red light. When the boys reached the crossing, a stream of traffic barred the way. Then a huge tanker halted for a left turn, completely blocking the intersection. By the time the route was clear, the getaway car was nowhere in sight.

"What luck!" Joe groaned.

The boys cruised around for a while, hoping to find the trail again, but finally gave up.

"Guess we may as well go back and get Chet," Frank sighed.

A police squad car was parked in front of the novelty shop. When the Hardys walked in, Mr Bivven was relating the details of the holdup to the officers.

"These are the boys," he said, nodding at Frank and Joe.

"Any luck tracing the thieves?" one of the officers asked.

Frank shook his head glumly. "We couldn't even get their licence number."

He gave a detailed description of the green saloon and also reported the general route which the thieves had taken.

"I'll put it on the radio right away," said the other policeman. "There's still a chance we can stop 'em before they get out of town." He hurried outside to the squad car.

The other officer took note of the names and

addresses of everyone involved, then left the shop.

"Too bad, Chet," Joe sympathized. "Looks as if you're out of luck for a dummy today."

"You're telling me," the young ventriloquist answered gloomily.

"Don't be too sure of that," put in Mr Bivven with a grin.

"Huh?" Chet's eyes popped. "What do you mean?"

"I mean there might just be another Hugo back in the storeroom. Dummies have been selling quickly, but while I was talking to those officers, I suddenly remembered tucking another box up on the top shelf. But don't get your hopes too high till I make sure."

Chet waited in eager suspense. A few moments later Mr Bivven reappeared, beaming triumphantly. "Yes! Got one right here."

"Hot ziggety!" Chet pounced on the box in delight, ripping off the cover. As he pulled out the dummy, both Frank and Joe gave a yelp of excitement.

This one wore a purple turban!

"My stars!" Mr Bivven chuckled. "Seems like you two are just as het-up as your friend here about finding this extra Hugo. But I reckon that's only natural, seeing as how you took your lives in your hands trying to save the other one."

Frank and Joe merely smiled and made no effort to explain their jubilation. But the same thought was passing through both their minds. Could this be the "Hugo purple turban" referred to in their father's message? And had the two men made off with the wrong dummy?

Meanwhile, Chet was putting the new Hugo through

its paces. "Boy, this is for me!" he gloated. "I'll work with it at home this evening!"

As the proprietor wrote out the receipt, Joe examined the dummy but could find nothing unusual about it. Frank again glanced at the instruction sheet. This one was also printed in the same three languages.

Suddenly Frank's eyes narrowed. "That's funny," he muttered under his breath.

"What's funny?" Joe asked.

"These directions. The ones in French and English are the same as those which came with the other dummy. But the directions in Spanish are different."

Both boys could read French and Spanish.

"You're sure?" Joe asked.

"Positive." After Mr Bivven finished writing out the receipt and tore off a copy for Chet, Frank asked the man, "Does any other store in Bayport sell the Huge dummies?"

"You'd like one too, eh?" The proprietor smiled. "Well, now, let me think." He paused and scratched his chin. "Might try Hanade's over on Bay Street."

"Hanade's?"

"That's right. Nice elederly Japanese. Runs a puppet-repair shop, and handles all kinds of interesting doodads."

The Hardys thanked him and left the store with Chet. Outside, their stout pal asked Frank why he was so interested in finding another dealer.

"Don't tell me you're going to take up ventriloquism too?" he teased.

"Not a chance," Frank replied, and explained about the curious difference in the instructions. He added

"It might be a fluke, or it might mean something. Anyhow, I'd like to check another set of instructions."

Hanade's Puppet Repair Shop did, indeed, carry "all kinds of doodads." The tiny store was crammed with Oriental trinkets, samurai swords, brass Buddhas, dolls' heads hanging on the wall, birds and bird cages, aquariums with darting tropical fish, and numerous other items.

Mr Hanade was a small, bespectacled, pleasant gentleman. "Ah, yes," he replied to Frank's question. "I carry the Hugo puppets. Made by a very fine company. Every puppet carefully inspected by owner before he sends it out. Which kind do you wish to see?"

"The model with a turban, like this one my friend has," replied Joe as Chet displayed his Hugo.

"You wait, please. I check."

Mr Hanade returned shortly with a box containing a Hugo similar to Chet's, but it wore a green turban. Ignoring the dummy, Frank took out the instruction sheet and compared it with the one in Chet's box.

"You're right," Joe muttered, reading over Frank's shoulder. "The Spanish wording *is* a little different!"

Frank asked if he might borrow Mr Hanade's sheet of instructions overnight, and offered to leave a dollar on deposit. Though puzzled, the man agreed politely.

"You take, please. No deposit necessary."

"Thank you," said Chet, and the boys left the shop.

Before dropping Chet at the farm, Joe said impulsively, "Say, fellows, do you think Professor Fox could be mixed up in anything shady?"

Chet declared that the TV performer had a fine

reputation, and he was sure that the man was above suspicion. Frank agreed with this.

That evening after supper Frank and Joe huddled around the study lamp in their room, with the two sets of instructions in front of them. They were identical in every way, except for the change in the Spanish wording.

"What do you make of it?" Joe asked his brother.

Frank furrowed his brow. "Might be some kind of a code. Let's compare all the word changes and see what we get."

They had barely started on this job when the hall telephone rang. Joe took the call.

"This is Chief Collig," came a crisp voice. "Understand you and your brother were at Bivven's Novelty Shop this afternoon when the owner got robbed."

"That's right. In fact, we chased the holdup men."

"Anything to do with a case your father's working on, Joe?"

"Could be, sir. We're not sure."

"Well, if you're interested, the place was robbed again tonight. Or, anyhow, it was broken into and ransacked."

"What!" Joe cried out.

"Happened just about twenty minutes ago," the chief went on. "An officer walking past heard some noises and figured something funny was going on. When he went to investigase, the burglars ducked out the back way."

"Thanks for the tip, Chief," Joe said. "Frank and I will go right over there."

Frank was equally startled when he heard about the

urglary. "I wonder if those men stole the wrong Hugo, nd came back for another try!"

"Sure sounds that way," Joe agreed, "but they must ave heard Mr Bivven say it was his last Hugo in ock."

The two boys drove through the darkened streets of ayport to the novelty shop on King Street. The store as ablaze with light, but no squad car stood at the cene. Apparently the police detectives had already left, ut there was an officer on guard at the door.

The Hardys identified themselves, and Frank added, Chief Collig just phoned us the news."

"He called me too," said the patrolman, and let them nter.

Mr Bivven was busy straightening up the shop. "Oh, 's you boys," he murmured, glancing up as the door's ell tinkled.

Most of the toys, dolls, and scale models had already een neatly replaced on the shelves.

"Sorry to hear the news, Mr Bivven," Frank said. 'Exactly what happened?"

The proprietor shrugged and sighed. "Place was ansacked but nothing taken. Dratted nuisance! urglars twice in one day! I just can't figure it out. till, I reckon I'm lucky it wasn't any worse."

"Mind if we look around for clues?" Frank asked.

"Go ahead, but the police have already done so."

As the boys poked about the shop, Mr Bivven bent lown behind the counter. A moment later he stood up.

"Now that's strange," he remarked with a puzzled rown. "Seems as though someone's been fiddling with ny sales slips."

"Sales slips!" Frank was struck by a sudden fear.

"Yes. Had 'em stashed away in order down here Now they're all messed up."

"Any missing?"

Mr Bivven scratched his bald head. "Well, now that's a mite hard to say without checking the cash register tape."

Frank said urgently, "Never mind the rest. Just look for the one you wrote up for our friend this afternoon The name was Morton—Chet Morton."

"Sure, sure, I remember. Let me see." Mr Bivven brought out the sheaf of slips, thumbed through them several times, then looked up in surprise. "By jing, that one's gone. Those burglars must have taken it!"

"That's what I guessed," Frank said. "They came back to check on who had purchased other dummies lately and found out Chet had one!"

"That means Chet's in danger!" Joe said grimly "And maybe Iola and their dad and mother!" Turning to Mr Bivven, he asked, "May I use your phone?"

"Sure thing."

Thoroughly alarmed by now, Joe scooped up the telephone and dialled Chet's number. At the other end of the line, he could hear a steady series of rings. But after a minute he gave up.

"No answer," he reported to Frank. "Come on Let's get out there fast!"

The boys dashed out of the shop, leaped into the convertible, and headed for the Morton farm. Once outside of town, Frank switched on the full beam head lights. The twin beams probed the darkness as they sped along.

Neither boy spoke, but both were gripped by the same fear. Was the Morton family in trouble? Why had no one answered the phone when Chet had said he would be at home?

Presently the farmhouse loomed up against the night sky. The windows were dark.

"I don't like this," Frank said grimly.

· 5 ·

A Startling Discovery

FRANK jammed on the brakes and the convertible lurched to a halt in the Mortons' driveway. The boys jumped out and sprinted up the front-porch steps.

As Joe rang the doorbell, Frank noticed that the front door stood slightly ajar.

"It's open!" he whispered.

Afraid of some danger, Frank and Joe cautiously entered the hall. Like all the rest of the house, the living room was shrouded in darkness. Frank, in the lead, groped for the light switch.

Joe's scalp bristled when he heard some faint whimpering noises. The sounds were muffled and scarcely seemed human.

Frank found the light switch and clicked it on. As the room leaped into brilliance, both boys exclaimed aloud.

Chet, Iola, and Mr and Mrs Morton were lying on the floor, bound and gagged!

"Jumpin' catfish!" Joe gulped.

The Hardys rushed forward and quickly started to untie the victims.

"Oh, my gracious! Thank you, thank you!" Chet's mother gasped as Frank removed her gag and undid the ropes.

"Luckily none of you were harmed, Mrs Morton," he replied. Gently he helped her to her feet and then to the sofa.

Chet, however, was not so grateful. "I thought you fellows promised me there wouldn't be any rough stuff on this case!" he grumbled while Joe worked on a knot.

"What happened?" Frank asked.

The story tumbled out in a confused babble as the whole Morton family gave the details. They had been watching a television show in their living room when two masked men burst in. The intruders had tied up the Mortons, then searched the house and made off with something tucked under one man's arm.

"I'm willing to bet they're the same ones who held up the novelty shop this afternoon," Chet asserted. "One was a tall man and the other short. The tall guy's ears stuck out!"

Frank and Joe looked at each other in dismay. "I guess that means they took Hugo," said Joe.

Frank nodded, then said to the Mortons, "Please check and make sure what was stolen."

The family scattered through the rooms of the rambling farmhouse to inspect the results of the burglary. Iola was the first to report.

"I know one thing they took!" she cried out, running downstairs from her bedroom.

"What?" asked Joe.

"One of my big puppets. It looked something like Chet's new dummy—even wore a purple turban."

"Of course!" Joe snapped his fingers. "I'll bet those burglars were in such a hurry that they grabbed the wrong doll!"

The boys' hopes soared, but Frank added cautiously, "Let's not count our chickens till we hear from Chet."

The words were hardly spoken when Chet came lumbering joyfully on to the scene. He was clutching Hugo in one hand. "Look! He's still here!" Chet gloated. "I had him stowed in my cupboard, inside a pillowcase, and those men passed it up!"

The boys let out a whoop of triumph. Then Joe put in a wry afterthought:

"Now all we have to do is find out why those thieves were so eager to get hold of Hugo."

While Frank telephoned a report to Chief Collig, Iola made hot cocoa for everyone. As they sat in the living room drinking it, Chet gulped down three cupfuls. Then he laid his cup and saucer aside and picked up Hugo.

"And now, ladies and gentlemen," the young ventriloquist announced, "we'll forget what happened and have a quick performance to show you what's to come later on my full-time television show!"

He set the dummy on his knee and proceeded to roll its huge popeyes from side to side. Then, as he manipulated Hugo's head and jaws, Chet went into his act. Many of his gags drew laughs from his audience.

Gaining confidence, Chet launched into a long, windy speech—at the same time working Hugo's head, arms, and legs in a wildly comical manner. Leaning forward with excitement, Chet grinned at his amused audience and perched the dummy on the edge of his knee.

Suddenly he jerked Hugo's limbs a bit too hard. The dummy slid off his knee and crashed to the floor, face down, amid a sound of shattering glass!

Chet went white. "Hugo!" he wailed mournfully. I've ruined you!"

Frank and Joe rushed forward to assay the damage. Don't worry," Joe consoled his friend. "It's not too ad."

"Those big, beautiful eyes—they're broken!" Chet roaned, kneeling on the floor.

"You can probably get new ones," Frank assured im. Cautiously he started picking up the glassy slivers nd fragments. "Gosh," he remarked, "those eyes were ven bigger than I—Oh, oh!"

"What's the matter?" asked Joe as Frank broke off vith a gasp of amazement.

"This stuff isn't glass—at least not all of it."

"Then what is it?" asked Chet.

Frank's voice quivered with excitement. "This may ound crazy, but I think some of these pieces are uncut iamonds!"

"*What!*" Everyone in the room jumped up in stonishment and clustered round Frank.

"D-did you say *diamonds?*" Chet stuttered.

"That's what they look like." Frank held up some of he stones, which resembled tiny, greasy pebbles.

"Are you sure?" Iola asked. "They don't sparkle nuch!"

"Rough stones look this way before they're cut," 'rank explained. "At least that's what I've read. What lo you think, Joe?"

His brother nodded. "I think you're right. And that xplains the burglaries. No wonder those men were so ager to grab Hugo!"

Picking up the dummy in one hand, Joe borrowed a

hair pin from Iola and began probing into the hollow
eye shells. Several more uncut diamonds came tumbling
out.

"I can't believe it!" Chet exclaimed. "Any more of
them?"

"No, but here's something else."

Joe extracted a tiny, rolled-up wad of paper. When
spread open, it revealed a strange printed notation:

Skeleton Rock 176

"How odd!" exclaimed Mrs Morton, and Iola
added, "It's positively spooky!"

Her father frowned uneasily. "Frank, you and Joe
have had experience with this sort of thing. What do
you think we should do?"

"If you don't mind, Mr Morton, I'd like to take both
the dummy and the diamonds home with us, so we can
investigate them further."

"All right, you do that!" From the tone of his voice,
Chet's father sounded relieved to have the disturbing
objects removed from his house before the thieves might
pay a return visit.

Before leaving, Frank telephoned his father's top
investigator, Sam Radley, and asked him to meet the
brothers at the Hardy home.

"I'll start at once," the detective promised.

Soon after the boys reached their house, they heard
Sam's car pull into the drive. Joe hurried to let him
in.

"What's up, boys?" asked the muscular, sandy-
haired detective as soon as he was seated in the living
room.

Frank briefed him quickly, then showed Sam the dummy and the curious-looking stones. The detective picked up one of the gems and held it to the light. Then he took a jeweller's eye-glass from his pocket and scrutinized the stone carefully.

"It's an uncut diamond, all right," Sam announced. He examined the others. "Several carats altogether; the lot of them should be worth a good sum of money." He advised the boys to notify Mr Hardy about their find as soon as possible.

Joe warmed up the short-wave radio transmitter and tuned to the Hardys' special frequency for secret communications. He spoke into the mike:

"Bayport calling Fenton H. in Puerto Rico! Come in, please!"

Again and again Joe repeated the call. But transmitting conditions were poor and he failed to make contact.

"Never mind," said Frank. "We'll try again tomorrow."

"Which reminds me," Sam Radley put in. "I have news for you two."

He reported that Jack Wayne had spotted a car, tent, and trailer which might belong to Hugo and Abdul. He had made the discovery while flying over a wooded area fifty miles away.

"He couldn't get any answer to a phone call here, so he contacted me," Sam explained. "Told me he was planning to take you up for a look-see at five tomorrow morning. He didn't think the trailer would pull out before that."

The boys were jubilant at the news, and called Jack

to say they would be on hand promptly for the take-off

Early the next morning Frank and Joe hopped out of bed the instant their alarm clock rang. After breakfast they drove to the airport.

Jack Wayne had his own plane, *Skyhappy Sal*, fuelled and ready on the runway. He was talking to Tony Prito, a good friend of the Hardy boys. During the summer the handsome, dark-eyed, olive-skinned boy drove a truck for his father's construction firm.

"Hi, fellows!" Tony greeted them. "Dad gave me the morning off. I decided to get some exercise and hike out here to see your dad's new plane. Boy, it's a real beauty. Say, you Hardys are on the job early. Another case?"

Frank explained briefly what their mission was, and Jack asked, "Want to come up with us? I have room for another passenger and we'll be back soon."

Tony enthusiastically accepted, and a few minutes later they took off. As the plane soared high above Bayport, Jack turned to Joe.

"Here, take over," the pilot said. "Might as well get a lesson out of this while you're in the air."

Joe was a good pilot and navigated the craft on a straight course towards the spot where Jack had sighted Hugo's trailer.

"We're getting close," Jack said as a wooded area came into view. "Drop down a little, Joe."

Soon Frank cried out. "There they are! That's Hugo's gear all right."

Joe swooped lower to get a better look at the fortune teller's camp. The drone of the plane's engine must have aroused the occupants, for a man came rushing out of the trailer.

"Abdul!" Frank exclaimed.

Shaking his fist, the giant rushed back into the trailer and emerged with a high-powered rifle.

"He's going to shoot at us!" Tony cried out.

"Take her up!" Jack ordered.

Joe began to climb for altitude. Seconds later there was a flash from the rifle muzzle. Almost at the same instant, sheets of flame billowed from under the engine cowling and smoke began to seep into the cabin.

"He's hit a fuel line!" Jack shouted. "The engine's on fire!"

· 6 ·

Musical Password

INSTINCTIVELY Joe pulled the controls back and lowered the wing into a steep left bank. He jammed the right rudder pedal to its full limit. The plane descended rapidly and skidded sideways in a "slip."

"Good work!" Jack said to Joe. "The plane's side motion will keep the flames away from the cabin!"

Joe reached down between the seats and turned the fuel selector valve to the "off" position, thus cutting off the flow of fuel from the tanks to the engine.

"Keep her slipping towards that clearing just to your left!" Jack ordered. "We should make it in there easily!" Joe nodded.

With the fuel valve turned off, the engine used the remaining petrol in the lines. It then sputtered and died.

Joe and his companions watched anxiously as the plane slipped towards the clearing. When just a few feet above it, the young pilot kicked the rudder pedal into neutral and levelled the wings. There was a jolt as he pulled the wheel back hard and the plane touched down on the grassy clearing. Joe then pressed hard on the wheel brakes. The craft rolled ahead for several yards and came to a halt with a lurch.

"Handled like a veteran!" Jack gave Joe a broad grin.

At that moment Frank caught sight of Abdul and Hugo sprinting towards their car. "Those men are getting away!" he yelled.

The Hardys and the others hopped out of the plane and dashed after them. But the men had too big a lead. They jumped into their car while the pursuers were still fifty yards away. The car roared down the woods road and disappeared.

Though disappointed, Frank pointed out that at least the suspects had had to abandon their tent and trailer. "Maybe they left some clues."

A quick search revealed little of interest. Besides some costumes, the crystal ball, and fortune-telling paraphernalia, Hugo and Abdul's gear consisted of food, street clothing, and cooking utensils. The searchers turned their attention to smaller articles.

"What's this?" Tony asked, unrolling a flag which he had found tucked away on a shelf of the trailer. On the left was a white circle on a red triangular field, and five green and white stripes running horizontally.

"A foreign flag!" Frank exclaimed.

"What about this?" Jack asked, pointing to a black cloth skeleton on the lower right-hand corner.

"Some kind of a Jolly Roger," Joe suggested.

"But why would petty thieves use a pirate flag?" Tony queried.

"Perhaps Hugo and Abdul belong to some rebel group," Frank mused.

Tony remarked, "Maybe they're just a couple of petty fakers."

Frank shook his head thoughtfully. "In that case, why all the rough stuff when we first saw them, and the rifle-shot just now? If you ask me, they're mixed up in something big—and this skeleton flag may be a clue."

The group headed back to *Skyhappy Sal*. Jack Wayne removed part of the cowling and made a quick examination of the damage caused by Abdul's bullet. The shot had almost severed the slender copper tubing of the fuel line.

"What's the verdict?" Frank inquired.

Jack shrugged, frowning. "I can make a temporary repair with a plastic line—good enough to get us in the air, anyhow. But I doubt that it would hold as far as Bayport."

"How about the Eastern City airport?" Tony suggested. "We could install a new fuel line there."

Jack nodded. "That's what we'll have to do."

He made the repair quickly, then everyone piled in. With Joe at the controls, the plane headed towards Eastern City. Located less than twenty miles away, this thriving city was a terminus for a number of airlines. Jack explained their plight to the tower and received permission to land. A mechanic guided him as he taxied the plane to a repair hangar.

"How long do you think it'll take to put in the new line?" Joe asked as they climbed out.

"Oh, not too long, once I get the right size of tubing," the pilot replied. "Fifteen, twenty minutes— if Tony will help me."

"Sure, be glad to!" Tony, an expert with tools, loved to tinker over an engine.

"In that case," said Frank, "Joe and I will find a phone booth and call the police."

They strode quickly to the terminal building. As they skirted the magazine stand on their way to the telephone booths, they noticed a man seated alone in a corner. Olive-skinned, with long, shiny black hair, he looked like a Latin American. The man slouched on the bench, chin in hand, listening to music which apparently was issuing from a small portable radio on his lap.

Joe grinned at the catchy tune. "Boy, I go for that stuff," he said.

"What stuff?" Frank asked.

"Hot calypso!" Joe said.

His reply seemed to electrify the man on the bench. Jumping to his feet, he darted towards the boy and hissed in his ear, "Where are your gloves, you fool? You might leave fingerprints."

Joe blinked and stared. The man's next move was even more astounding. He pulled a pair of gloves from his pocket and stuffed them into Joe's hand!

The boy was taken completely by surprise, but instinct warned him not to betray his reaction. The stranger watched him closely.

Joe swallowed hard and looked at the gloves. They were made of grey fabric with a small label sewn to the hem of one, reading *Made in Tropicale*. Acting on a hunch, Joe pulled them on.

This seemed to please the stranger, who gave a tight smile. "Ah, *bueno!*" He produced a small key and slipped it into Joe's gloved hand, adding, "You have been instructed!"

Without another word the man turned, switched off the music, and strode away. For the first time, Frank and Joe noticed that what they had thought was a portable radio was actually a small portable record-player.

"Let's follow him!" Joe said.

"Better not," Frank advised. "I think we've stumbled on to something big. We've done the right thing so far. Let's not spoil it."

"You're right. 'Hot calypso' must be a password. Let's look at this key."

Joe held it up for examination. The key was inscribed with the number 176.

Frank repeated the number excitedly. "That note we found in the dummy's eye!" he exclaimed. "It said 'Skeleton Rock 176'!"

"But what does it stand for?" Joe asked.

Frank thought a moment. "I can't answer that, but I'll bet this key opens one of those public lockers over there."

The boys hurried to the south wall of the air terminal, honeycombed with metal lockers.

"Here it is," said Frank.

Joe glanced around cautiously. The Latin American was not in sight and no one else seemed to be looking at the boys. Joe inserted the key in the lock. *It fitted!*

He turned the key and the door swung open. The locker contained a black-leather zipped case.

Joe reached in and pulled out the case. The next instant, both boys jumped in alarm as a voice behind them barked:

"You're under arrest!"

·7·

Twin Clues

As THE Hardys whirled round from the airport lockers, they saw a dark-haired, hard-jawed man of medium build eyeing them coldly.

He flipped open his coat and flashed a detective's badge. "Now, then, who are you and what's your game?"

"We're Frank and Joe Hardy," Frank said coolly. "Our father is Fenton Hardy, the investigator. While we're at it, maybe you wouldn't mind telling us who *you* are?"

"Shanley, airport detective!" the man replied crisply. Opening his wallet, he showed them his detective's licence. "You two still haven't told me what you're up to," he prodded.

"We're not 'up to' anything," Joe said tersely.

Shanley was annoyed. "Let's have a look at that leather case," he demanded.

But Frank interposed. "If you want to see the contents, let's go to police headquarters."

"Okay," the detective grumbled. "Come on. We'll go in my car."

The Hardys agreed and the trio headed out through the glass doors of the terminal building, with Joe clutching the briefcase.

"Car's over there at the far end of the car park." Shanley pointed.

As they started across the parking area, Joe caught his brother's eye. He made a slight gesture towards the zipped case. Frank nodded.

Turning to Shanley, Frank started chattering casually. "Do you have an office here in Eastern City?" he inquired.

While Frank distracted the detective's attention, Joe gave the zip a quick jerk. Inside, he caught a glimpse of several thin, flat boxes sealed in cellophane. They bore a drug manufacturer's label with the name *Variotrycin.*

Joe pulled the zip shut before Shanley noticed anything. The young detective's mind was racing.

"Variotrycin's that new wonder drug I read about in the papers," Joe thought. "But what has a new wonder drug to do with dummies and diamonds—or *Skeleton Rock 176?*"

Joe, deeply engrossed in trying to find an answer to the puzzle, was taken off guard by three men who suddenly darted out from between two cars parked nearby.

"We'll take that case!" snarled the leader, a burly, baldheaded man in a polo shirt.

"Oh, no, you won't!" Joe ducked, and threw up an arm to protect himself.

Frank leaped to his assistance, fists flying, as the hoodlums tried to grab the case.

To their astonishment, Shanley had disappeared. But there was no time to speculate about what had happened to him as Frank drove home a punch that split the lip of his adversary, while Joe gave another of the men a blow that sent him reeling.

In doing so, Joe dropped the case he had held under his left arm. As the young detective stooped to pick it up, he was amazed to have it snatched from the ground by none other than Shanley! The detective had crept up from behind.

"Thanks!" Shanley sneered, and sprinted for his car.

The Hardys were powerless to stop him. With the odds three against two, their attackers were pressing the boys harder than before.

Furiously, Frank and Joe swung their fists with telling effect. One of their opponents howled with pain as Joe caught him on the nose. A second later the baldheaded leader winced and groaned under the walloping impact of Frank's fist under his chin.

Even so, the fight began to go against the boys. Step by step, they were being driven back and hemmed in against the bumper of a parked car.

Then, suddenly, the tide of battle turned. The burly baldheaded man was jerked round and struck on the jaw by a blow that rocked him on his heels.

"Tony!" Joe cheered. Heartened by the unexpected help, the Hardys put forth a fresh surge of fighting fury.

Their assailants lost heart rapidly. "These guys are too tough! I'm gettin' outta here!" gasped one of the ruffians. Pulling loose from the fray, he turned and ran, with Tony after him.

The baldheaded ringleader followed, with Frank at his heels. As the third hoodlum tried to join in the getaway, Joe dropped him with a flying tackle.

But the leader and the other ruffian kicked off their pursuers and leaped into a car that was waiting for them on the road beyond the parking area. At the wheel was Shanley!

Discouraged by this latest development, Frank and Tony went back to Joe, who was holding their prisoner. The fellow was bony and pinched-faced, and wore a cheap-looking pinstriped suit.

"We're taking you to police headquarters," Joe told him.

The sullen man shifted uneasily, but kept quiet as the group headed for the taxi stand.

"By the way, fellows," said Tony, "would you mind telling me what this is all about?"

Frank gave him a quick account of the phony detective and the unexpected attack. "Thanks for coming to our rescue. You really saved the day!"

"Ditto!" put in Joe. "If it hadn't been for you, we wouldn't have this prisoner. By the way, Tony, you'd better go tell Jack Wayne what happened. We'll be back soon."

"Okay," Tony agreed. "But don't let buster boy here pull any more fast ones!"

As he headed back to the hangar, Frank and Joe hustled their prisoner into one of the waiting taxis.

"Police headquarters," Frank directed the driver.

A few minutes later the taxi stopped in front of the brick building.

The sergeant in charge led the Hardys and their prisoner into the office of Inspector Moon, a friend of Fenton Hardy. He greeted the boys warmly, then said to a detective, "Take this man into the interrogation room and get the facts." Inspector Moon turned back to Frank and Joe. "Now give me the whole story."

The boys related everything that had happened at the airport terminal, including the way Shanley had led them into an ambush and then stolen the leather case.

"What did Shanley look like?" the officer asked. As Frank gave a description of the man, the inspector frowned and shook his head. "That wasn't Shanley."

"He was impersonating him, you mean?" Frank asked. "We saw his detective's licence."

"Sure, *they* were the real Shanley's all right. His house was broken into last night and all his credentials stolen," the inspector explained.

Frank and Joe asked to read the report of the robbery, but found no clues of interest. In answer to Inspector Moon's questions, they explained that they were helping their father on a case and described their brush with Hugo and Abdul at the wooded site.

"I'll put out a call for them right away," Inspector Moon said. He picked up his phone and ordered that an alarm be sent to all radio cars.

"One thing I don't understand is why that Latin American fellow at the airport slipped me the gloves and key," said Joe, after the officer hung up. "Couldn't he tell just by looking at me that I wasn't the right guy?"

"Maybe you *do* look like the right guy," Inspector Moon pointed out.

"Wow! I never thought of that!"

Despite the seriousness of the situation, Frank suddenly grinned. "Good grief! My brother looking like some underworld character!" Then he sobered. "If this is some kind of a racket—like a theft ring for passing stolen goods—we now have a good description of one of the members."

"Right," the inspector agreed. "I'll pass the word round for the men to be on the lookout for a fellow answering Joe's description."

"But of the criminal type, please," Joe pleaded.

Just then the door of the interrogation room opened, and the plainclothesman came out with the prisoner.

"Learn anything?" Inspector Moon asked the detective.

"No," he replied. "He won't even tell us his name."

"Any identification?" the inspector queried.

"Not even a driver's licence. Only thing that might help is this tattoo." The detective pulled up the prisoner's sleeve to show a pineapple tattoo on his left forearm.

"Hmm. It's not much to go on," the inspector said, "but check the files. Anything else?"

"Yes, sir. This prisoner was carrying these in his pocket, together with a ticket to Mexico."

With a baffled look, the detective held up a pair of doll's glass eyes! Instantly the Hardys realized they were just like the dummy's eyes which had contained uncut diamonds!

· 8 ·

Spanish Code

FRANK and Joe were excited. Here was a definite clue that tied the Eastern City holdup men to the Hugo dummy racket!

"I'd like to speak to you privately," Frank said to the police inspector. "And bring the doll's eyes along, please."

When they were alone in a rear office, Frank declared, "These doll's eyes prove the man you're holding and his gang are mixed up in the case Dad's working on!"

"And what about the boxes of Variotrycin in the briefcase?" Joe asked.

Inspector Moon looked thoughtfully at both boys and said that he would follow through on this angle in a few minutes, then he held up the doll's eyes to the light.

"No diamonds here," he announced. "These eyes are empty. But we still have plenty to hold Mr Pineapple on. Maybe he'll change his mind later about talking."

Inspector Moon asked the boys to wait while he tried to find out about the Variotrycin. He telephoned first to Watkins Pharmacy. The boys could hear both sides of the conversation.

"That stuff's pretty new," Mr Watkins told the

inspector, "and very expensive. Far as I know, the Lexo Drug people that make it won't be supplying it in quantity until they can lower the price."

"Where is Lexo Drug?"

Mr Watkins said the company had a factory in Hartsburg. "If you have a prescription, I could put in a special order—"

"No, thanks," the inspector interrupted.

Hartsburg was less than a hundred miles from Bayport. Inspector Moon then placed a long-distance call to the company.

"I'd like to speak to the plant manager," he told the switchboard girl.

A man's gruff voice came on the line. "McCardle speaking."

Inspector Moon introduced himself and said, "I'm calling to find out if any shipments of Variotrycin have been stolen recently."

The plant manager asked with a sharp note of interest, "Who did you say you were?"

"Inspector Moon of the Eastern City Police Department."

Mr McCardle cleared his throat, then said that a special messenger carrying a consignment of their new product had been attacked and robbed late the day before.

"Where?"

"Not far from here."

"Have you contacted your local police?" Inspector Moon asked.

"No. We just heard about the robbery. But I'll do so right away," McCardle replied.

He asked why the inspector had called him, and was old about the boxes in the brief case. "Well, we hope hat you find the thief!" the manager said, then said goodbye.

Inspector Moon turned to the Hardys. "How about you fellows helping on this?"

"We will!" the young sleuths promised.

Before leaving headquarters, Frank asked if he and his brother might borrow the doll eyes for further examination. Inspector Moon readily agreed.

The boys took a taxi back to the airport. Before they took off for Bayport, Tony telephoned his father to tell what had happened. As he returned to the others, he said, "Lucky break! Dad says I can have the rest of the day off!"

On the flight back, the Hardys brought Jack and Tony up to date on the developments in the mystery.

"Things certainly worked fast," Jack remarked.

"Yes, and thanks a lot for your help," Joe said as they landed at Bayport. Frank echoed his words.

The pilot grinned. "Any time, fellows."

As the boys drove off, Joe suggested that they stop at Mr Hanade's puppet-repair shop to see if he could tell them anything about the glass eyes, and to return his instruction sheet, which they had copied.

A few minutes later the trio pulled up outside Mr Hanade's shop. The pleasant Japanese proprietor greeted the Hardys and Tony politely. "You learn something from instruction sheet for Hugo dummy?" he asked as Joe thanked him for lending it to them.

"Not yet, but we have something to show you," Joe

replied. He took out the glass eyes. "Ever seen any like these before?"

Hanade studied them curiously. "Very old," he murmured. "Nowadays, manufacturers do not make dolls' eyes like this. Too expensive to make out of coloured glass. Besides, glass breaks too easily."

He explained that eyes for modern dolls are normally made of plastic with a metal rod running through them. The rod is usually hinged, with a small counterweight to make the eyes open and close.

Frank murmured to Joe, "With a rod running through them, there wouldn't be much room inside for hiding anything."

Joe nodded and said aloud, "If they're plastic, they're probably solid instead of hollow."

"That is correct," said Mr Hanade.

"Do your Hugo dummies have solid plastic eyes?" Frank queried.

"Yes. Modern merchandise, of course."

"Any idea where these glass eyes might have come from?" Joe went on.

"Would be hard to say. Most likely from some old-fashioned American dolls or puppets."

"One more question," said Frank. "Where are the Hugo dummies made?"

"Mexico," said Mr Hanade. At once the boys thought of the prisoner who had a ticket to Mexico. The man went on, "The dummies are fashioned of papier-mâché."

The boys thanked him for his help and left. As they drove home, the group exchanged views on the mystery.

"I still can't figure out why those guys in Eastern City were so anxious to get their hands on that Variotrycin," Joe remarked. "Maybe there's a connection between the drugs and the diamonds."

"And how about that pirate flag in Abdul's trailer?" Tony reminded them. "Where does that come in?"

Frank shrugged. "You've got me pal!"

When they reached the Hardy home, Chet Morton was rocking himself in the chair on the front porch.

"Hey, watch it, pal! You want that thing to collapse?" Joe called out laughingly.

"Where've you fellows been?" Chet complained. "I've been waiting here so long I'll bet I've missed my lunch."

Frank sniffed the appetizing aroma of freshly baked cake that floated out through the open windows. "Better come in and eat with us, Chet."

The stout teenager needed no urging. Soon all four boys were seated round the dining-room table, with Mrs Hardy and Aunt Gertrude, spooning up hearty servings of delicious onion soup and enjoying crusty French bread.

"How did things go, boys?" Mrs Hardy asked.

After hearing all about the exciting adventures, both women gasped and Aunt Gertrude said, "I warned you! If you'd only pay attention to me, you wouldn't risk your lives that way."

Mrs Hardy looked troubled. "Please be careful," she cautioned.

After lunch the four boys trooped upstairs to Frank and Joe's room. Once again the young sleuths took out the two instruction sheets for the Hugo dummies and began to compare them.

"I'll read off the extra words included on Chet's sheet that are different, Frank, and you write them down," Joe suggested.

"Okay, shoot!"

Frank wrote the words in a column with the translation opposite each one:

Cuerpo	body
ahora	now
bajo	low or under
escena	stage, scene
zapato	shoe
ojo	eye
necesitar	to want or need
aqui	here
Número	number

"What is it—a code?" asked Tony.

"Perhaps," said Frank. After a couple of minutes of trying various combinations, he added, "I can't make any sense out of them."

"Let's try the first letters of each Spanish word reading down," suggested Joe. "C,a,b,e,z,o,n,a,n—"

"The first word, *Cuerpo*," said Tony, "and the last word, *Número*, both have capital letters. Maybe that means the N should be separated from the rest."

Frank wrote it down this way:

CABEZONA N

"I believe you're right," he commented, and consulted a Spanish dictionary. He read aloud:

" 'Cabezon, na, *adj. big-headed; stubborn; n. collar of a shirt; opening in a garment for the passage of the head; noseband (for horses).' "

"Doesn't make sense to me," said Frank, "unless the code refers to the Hugo dummy's big head."

"That's it!" Joe exclaimed. "The instructions might point out that the diamonds were secreted in the dummy's head! And the N could stand for *north*, which is in fact where the dummy's eyes are placed on its face."

Excited, the boys warmed up their short-wave radio and beamed out a call over the Hardys' special frequency. After several minutes Mr Hardy answered.

"Fenton to Bayport. Can you read me?"

"Sure can, Dad!" Joe replied into the mike. "We have some important news for you!"

"Better not tell it now," Mr Hardy warned hastily. "Someone may be listening!"

"Then tell us where to reach you and we'll send it in code by airmail," Joe told his father.

"I have a better idea, son. Suppose you and Frank fly down here to Puerto Rico and join me. I can use your help. Call Jack Wayne right away and make the arrangements."

Chet and Tony had listened to the invitation with envy. "Ask your dad if he can use us," said Chet. "We could be a big help!"

"It sure would be a lot of fun," Joe agreed.

"It's okay. Bring your pals along." Mr Hardy chuckled, having heard the whole conversation.

At once Chet and Tony dashed to the hall phone to call their parents. First Chet received permission to take a break from his summer work on the farm, then Tony's father agreed to give him time off.

The boys were jubilantly talking over their plans when the telephone rang sharply. It was Inspector Moon calling from Eastern City.

"I have some bad news," he told Joe, who answered. "That prisoner you and your brother captured this morning has just escaped by overpowering a guard."

"*Escaped!*" Joe echoed.

"I thought I'd better warn you two," the officer said.

"Thanks, Inspector. We'll be on our guard."

Frank was gravely alarmed when he learned of the escape. "Now we're in real trouble," he pointed out. "That man will pass along word to the gang that we have valuable information and they may try to harm us!"

"Good grief!" Joe exclaimed. "If they come here while we're gone, Mother and Aunt Gertrude will be in danger!"

"We'd better call Sam Radley and ask him to guard the house," Frank decided.

Mr Hardy's investigator readily agreed not only to stand guard himself at night, but to provide round-the-clock protection for the Hardy home. A call to Jack Wayne brought the promise that Mr Hardy's new six-seater cabin plane would be fuelled and ready for take-off at six the next morning.

"I'll be there at five to have everything in order," the pilot promised.

At dawn the brothers bounced out of bed, showered dressed hastily, and had a quick breakfast.

"Now take your time and chew your food properly,"

Aunt Gertrude told them tartly. "I doubt that the island of Puerto Rico will sink out of sight if you don't get there in the next few hours!"

After goodbyes and warnings to be careful, the boys flung their suitcases into the convertible and drove off. They picked up Chet and Tony, then set off for the airport.

It was a few minutes before six, and shreds of morning mist still clung to the ground when they arrived at the airport. Jack Wayne was nowhere in sight. A mechanic was refuelling the blue-and-white Hardy plane. The young detectives approached and asked him if he had seen Jack Wayne.

"I did, just a little while ago," the mechanic answered. "The last time I saw him he was heading for Hangar B. He asked me if I'd help him tow your father's plane out and refuel it. When I went over to the hangar a few minutes later, Jack was nowhere near. So I just went ahead and towed the plane out on my own."

The boys waited anxiously, but twenty minutes later, their pilot still had not arrived.

Frank's face clouded with worry. "I'm afraid that something has happened to Jack. He'd never be this late without letting me know."

"Yes," said Joe. "It looks as if our enemies may have already started their newest attack."

· 9 ·

The Ticking Suitcase

"MAYBE Jack went to the shop to get something," Tony said.

In pairs the boys began their hunt. When they met again a short time later, their faces registered failure.

"I'll call the motel where Jack lives," Frank decided. "He might have gone to his room to get something."

Hopefully the four boys hurried to the waiting room. Frank made the call.

"Is he there?" Joe asked anxiously when his brother emerged from the booth.

Frank shook his head. "The manager said Jack left a couple of hours ago."

For a moment the boys were silent, wondering what their next move should be. Suddenly Joe snapped his fingers. "We haven't checked Jack's plane. Let's go and look!"

With quick strides the boys headed for Hangar B, where their father and Jack kept their planes. Jack's sleek, silver-winged craft stood in one corner of the big corrugated-iron building.

Frank reached the plane first, climbed up, and jerked open the cabin door. He stopped short and gasped. Slumped on the floor was the huddled form of Jack Wayne!

"He's here, unconscious!" Frank reported.

"Good grief!" cried Joe.

Gently the boys lifted the pilot out of the plane and laid him on a pile of tarpaulins.

"Is he badly hurt?" Chet asked.

"I don't think so," Frank replied, taking Jack's pulse, which was even. "Just knocked out. In fact, I believe I smell chloroform in here."

Jack moaned and stirred. "Thank goodness it's nothing worse," said Joe.

A few minutes later, though still woozy, Jack was able to sit up. "W-what—? W-where—?" he murmured, shaking his head from side to side.

"Take it easy," Frank advised.

"Oh, hello, fellows," Jack said shakily.

Chet Morton brought him a drink of water. While the pilot was sipping it, Frank and Joe went off to question the man in charge of the airport at the time, Burt Hildreth.

"Did you notice strangers prowling around early this morning?"

"Don't recall seeing any," said Hildreth, a tall man with a weather-beaten face. "In fact, no one's been out to the field this morning—except when this young man showed up at five o'clock." He pointed to Joe.

"Me?"

"Sure. Don't tell me you've forgotten our conversation."

Frank and Joe looked at each other, startled.

The early-morning visitor to the airfield must have been the one who resembled Joe—the contact man for the theft ring!

Hildreth was puzzled. "What goes on here?" he

asked. "Are you fellows mixed up in some mystery?"

"Yes," said Frank. "Joe and I didn't arrive until a few minutes ago." He explained that the police were looking for a suspect who resembled Joe. He might even be made up to look like him.

"Well, I'll be doggoned!" Hildreth exclaimed. "That fellow sure is your double! He asked if Wayne had filed the take-off time for your flight. I said, 'No, not yet, but he told me last night you'd be leaving around six.' Then he walked off towards the hangar."

Joe's eyes widened as a frightening thought struck him. "I have a hunch we'd better check our plane and check it thoroughly!"

The boys hurried back to the hangar, where they found Jack Wayne fully recovered. He told them he had been about to step into the Hardy plane when someone had sneaked up behind him and clamped a chloroformed rag under his nose.

"That's the last I remember. But why would anyone want to knock me out?"

"So he could sabotage our plane before take-off!" Frank replied grimly, and related Hildreth's story.

"Great heavens!" exclaimed Jack. "If that's the deal, we'd better go over the ship with a fine-toothed comb, or we may wind up in the drink!"

Worried, the group towed the big blue-and-white craft out on to the hangar apron. Under Jack's supervision, they began a thorough check.

Engine, landing gear, control cables, elevators, ailerons, trim tabs—everything seemed to be in order. Even the radio and flight instruments showed no signs of tampering.

Frank relaxed a bit. "I guess my hunch was wrong. Anyhow, I'm glad we made sure."

"But we still don't know why Jack was attacked," Joe pointed out.

While the pilot went off to file his flight plan, the others refreshed themselves with some hot cocoa at the airport snack bar. Later, as Jack warmed up the engine for take-off, the boys lugged their baggage out to the plane.

Frank squatted just inside the cargo compartment in the rear of the plane and checked off each item as the others passed them in to him.

"Two bags for Joe and me," he sang out. "Three bags for Chet. One suitcase for Tony, and a bag and two suitcases for Jack already stowed aboard!"

Jack turned around. "Hey, did you say three for me? I brought only two."

"I'll bet Chet slipped in an extra one full of food!" Tony joked.

"Either that, or he's trying to sneak his dummy aboard as a stowaway." Joe chuckled.

Suddenly Frank turned pale. "Say, what if that fellow who chloroformed Jack planted the extra bag! It could mean—"

The pilot had already jumped up from his seat and hurried aft. "These are my two suitcases," he said, pointing them out.

Frank grabbed the extra bag from the cargo space and held it to his ear.

"It's ticking!" he cried. "A time bomb!"

There was an instant of near panic as Jack and the boys stood frozen with fear. Should they leap from the plane and leave it to blow up when the bomb went off? Or should they take a chance and try to carry the bag to a safe distance?

Frank glanced at his watch. It was 6.33. "The person who planted the bomb probably figured we wouldn't be airborne just yet, so the bomb must be set to explode a few minutes from now. Out of my way, boys!" he cried.

Before anyone could stop him, Frank jumped from the plane, bag in hand, and sprinted down the runway. Near the edge of the field, he paused and hurled the bag towards a vacant, brush-covered area beyond.

He was halfway back to the plane when the whole airport rocked under a sudden explosion. Frank was hurled to the ground by the tremendous blast. Joe and the others ran to help him as dirt, brush, and debris rained down on all sides of the blast area.

"Frank! Are you all right?" Joe cried, reaching his brother and kneeling down beside him.

"Sure. Just a little shaken up."

"And m-me too!" said Chet. "Man alive, I thought you were a goner!" The stout boy's face was ash white and the rest of the group looked equally shocked.

By this time, the airport was in an uproar and it was some time before everyone was reassured that the bomb planter had directed his venom only towards the Hardys.

Meanwhile, Frank made a full report over the phone to Chief Collig. Finally a signal for departure was given and the graceful blue-and-white plane took off on its flight to Puerto Rico.

Everyone relaxed as the plane headed out over the

Atlantic. The boys sat quietly and thought about the case. What sort of a racket were they up against? Obviously its members would stop at nothing to gain their objectives. The young sleuths had already had enough close scrapes to be sure of that!

Frank and Joe each took turns at the controls as Jack was still feeling the effects of the attack. It was nearing lunch-time when a voice came crackling over the plane's radio navigation frequency.

"*Sky Sleuth* One-One-Eight-Howe-Baker! This is Tancho radio! Do you read?"

Frank clicked the plane's transmitter to the proper frequency. He then picked up the microphone and spoke into it. "Tancho radio! This is *Sky Sleuth* One-One-Eight-Howe-Baker! Read you loud and clear! Go ahead!"

"Eight-Howe-Baker! This is Tancho radio! Bayport tower has requested us to convey a message to you from Mrs Hardy! You are requested to land at Centro in Tropicale! Repeat—land at Centro in Tropicale! Over!"

The boys were puzzled. Why land at the new Caribbean island democracy? Frank decided to check.

"Tancho radio! This is Eight-Howe-Baker! Would you please contact Bayport tower and have them call Mrs Hardy? We would like to verify that message!"

"Stand by!"

Several minutes passed before the communicator's voice again crackled from the loudspeaker.

"Eight-Howe-Baker! This is Tancho radio! Bayport tower reports they called your home! No answer! Can we be of further assistance? Over!"

"This is Eight-Howe-Baker! Negative! We are proceeding to Centro. Please change our flight plan accordingly! Over and out!"

Shifting course to the right, Jack headed southwest towards Tropicale. Finally the lush green shores of the island came into view. The pilot consulted a map as they flew inland and soon they sighted the bustling city of Centro.

Arrowing in towards the airfield on the outskirts of town, Jack cleared with the tower and made a smooth landing. Almost before the plane rolled to a stop, a man in a white suit came running out to meet them. He was tall and dark with a long, drooping moustache.

As the boys climbed out of the plane, the stranger shoved a note into Frank's hand, then dashed off the field. Puzzled, Frank unfolded the paper and read the typewritten message. It said:

> Danger. Do not come.
> Dad

Cross Fire

CHET groaned in dismay at Mr Hardy's message. To have come all this way and not go on to Puerto Rico!

Jack had a different idea. "Maybe it's a trick," he suggested.

"Yes, and the radio message too," Frank agreed.

"Then let's find that guy and make him talk!" Joe urged.

"Okay. Anybody see where he went?" Frank asked.

He and the others stared around the field. With several airliners loading and discharging passengers, the place throbbed with activity. Tourists swarmed about the terminal building.

"There he is!" cried Tony, pointing to a tall figure in a white suit talking earnestly to a group of men. They were standing near the road that bordered the field.

Joe took off at a fast sprint. All the others but Jack raced after him. As the boys ran, they caught a stir of movement in other parts of the field. Several uniformed men were pushing through the throng of people.

Suddenly a shot rang out, then another! The white-suited man and his companions jerked round, their hands flying towards their hip pockets.

"*La policia!*" one of them shouted.

Whipping out revolvers and automatics, they began

shooting back. In an instant the Hardys and their friends found themselves caught in a fusillade of cross fire as bullets whined back and forth through the air.

"Wow!" Tony exclaimed as one whistled close to his ear.

"We've walked into a war!" Chet wailed.

Following Joe and Frank's example, the others fanned out, but kept on running—in an effort to escape the deadly exchange and catch up to the deliverer of the note.

One of the gunmen spotted the Americans. He let out a sharp cry in Spanish, which seemed to throw his companions into a panic. The men ran towards two parked cars.

Bringing up the rear was the moutachioed man in the white suit who had delivered the note. Joe was now within a couple of yards of him. With a lunge the boy hurled himself in a fierce flying tackle. The white-suited man went down with a thud.

The other gunmen, already in the parked cars, made no effort to rescue their comrade. They sped off in a cloud of exhaust fumes!

By this time, the police had reached the scene in jeeps to give chase. But a lieutenant and several others stayed behind to take over the prisoner from the Americans.

"*Caramba*, señores!" the lieutenant exclaimed to Frank and Joe. "You are brave young men to capture unarmed, such a gunman. In fact, you are all brave señores and I offer you my thanks!"

"Glad to help, but who are these men?" Frank asked.

"Rebels plotting against the Tropicale Government," said the lieutenant. "But if you will be so kind, you will tell me why you were mixed up in this."

Frank told his story briefly and the officer urged the boys to accompany him to police headquarters and repeat what had happened.

When they arrived at headquarters, he introduced them to Lieutenant Garcia and once more the boys told their story. Before the officer could take action, five other members of the rebel group were brought in, two of them injured. One of the getaway cars had smashed into a lamppost while making a turn. All the occupants had been captured.

"A bad business, señores! You see, there have been several uprisings lately," Lieutenant Garcia explained to the Hardys. "The first took place at Santia, on the southeast coast of our island, but each new raid occurs farther west. We fear the rebels may be moving towards Savango."

He explained that the police had learned only a few hours earlier about the group's latest plan to seize or blow up the airport.

"But why?" Frank asked. "What's their purpose?"

The lieutenant shrugged. "*Quién sabe?* Perhaps they are criminals, crazy for power, trying to overthrow the lawfully elected government."

Meanwhile, the prisoners were being questioned in another room. Frank and Joe were allowed to be present at the interrogation. It was disappointing, because none of the captured men would talk.

"I'll bet the one we caught won't tell *us* anything, either," Joe whispered to his brother.

As Frank nodded, the man suddenly raised his hand to mop the sweat from his brow. Joe gasped and clutched his brother by the arm.

"Look!" he whispered.

On the prisoner's left forearm, just above the wrist, was a pineapple tattoo!

The Hardys exchanged excited glances. Did this sign mean that the man was a member of the same racket as the one in Eastern City with the tattoo on the left arm? The boys decided the chances were too slim for them to mention their suspicion to the Tropicale police.

After the prisoner had been taken to a cell, Lieutenant Garcia turned to the Hardys and said, "May I see the note, please, that was handed to you on the field?"

When the officer finished studying it, Frank added, "I have a hunch the radio message we got in the plane was a fake, but I'd like to make sure."

He asked permission to place a long-distance telephone call to Bayport. In a few minutes Mr. Hardy's voice came through.

"Is everything all right?" she asked quickly.

"There's nothing to worry about, Mother," Frank reassured her, then asked if she had sent the radio message.

"Why, no, son."

Somewhat upset, Mrs Hardy begged her sons to take care of themselves. "And that goes for Chet and Tony and Jack!" she added.

When Lieutenant Garcia heard Frank's report, he frowned. "It would appear, señores, that this gang was trying to lure you into some kind of trap. Fortunately their plan failed."

He summoned the prisoner who had delivered the note. The man glibly said a stranger had asked him to do the errand. Frank and Joe were sure he was lying, but he refused to change his story and was taken away to a cell.

After making signed statements, the Hardys were driven back to the airport in a police car. Here they ate a hearty lunch, then took off again for Puerto Rico.

"I certainly hope we have no more delays," Joe said, heaving a great sigh.

It was late afternoon when they came in sight of the beautiful Caribbean island. From the air, it looked like a paradise of emerald green. White beaches with waving palms rimmed the shore line. Farther inland, cool blue mountains reared upward from the coastal plain.

"Ah me! What a place in which to relax and dream!" Chet said as he peered down from the cabin window.

"You mean with a well-filled lunch basket?" Tony put in, chuckling.

To the southeast of the International Airport near San Juan a green-clad mountain peak soared against the sky. "That's *El Yunque*—The Anvil," Jack pointed out. "It's a tropical rain forest with ferns as high as houses."

They landed and admired the large white modern terminal building as they walked towards it. The structure seemed to be poised on stilts.

Mr Hardy was waiting to greet the travellers as soon as they cleared customs. "Good flight?" he asked.

"Wait'll you hear!" Joe grinned. "We stopped off in Tropicale and barged smack into a revolution!"

"Well, I'm glad you came through it alive!" Though eager to hear all the news, Mr Hardy cautioned everyone not to talk freely until they were in their hotel rooms.

The group managed to squeeze into a single taxi. Soon they were whisked through a beautiful residential area of pink and white villas, then out on to a wide boulevard lined by palms, in clear view of the sea.

"Pretty nice place," Chet remarked. "Let's have some fun while we're here and not get mixed up with a bunch of crooks."

The others smiled. When they reached the hotel, the boys went at once to Mr Hardy's room for a conference.

Frank and Joe quickly related everything that had happened to them since receiving his message of "Find Hugo purple turban."

Mr Hardy was amazed. "So there were diamonds in the dummy! This case is even more complex than I realized," he declared, his face grave. "And you've done a good job. I thought that message might be a clue to a smuggling racket. It was written on a piece of paper left in a hastily vacated house."

The detective confided to the boys that he was working for the United States Government on the theft of some rare isotopes—materials which could be used in the manufacture of atomic weapons.

"The FBI believes they were stolen here in Puerto Rico, en route to foreign countries," he added. "It looks as if we may be up against a gang of air-freight thieves and smugglers who deal in other things besides isotopes!"

"Any leads so far?" Frank asked.

"Just one. My next job is to keep watch at a freight warehouse near the airport."

Joe jumped up from his chair in excitement. "How about Frank and Chet and Tony and myself doing a stakeout at the warehouse?"

The other boys were equally enthusiastic about the idea, and Mr Hardy finally agreed. They soon devised a plan. The boys would hide in crates to be carted to the warehouse that evening.

After dinner the boys started out for a haulage company on a street called Calle Pacheco. The owner of the firm was cooperating with the police on the freight robberies.

"Don't look now," said Tony a few minutes later, "but I think a car's tailing us."

Frank leaned forward to watch the taxi's rear-view mirror. "You're right," he muttered. "Maybe we'd better split up."

Quickly he arranged with Chet and Tony to stay in the taxi and try to shake off their pursuer. "If you lose him, meet us at the haulage company in half an hour."

Farther down, the driver had to stop for a red light. Quickly the Hardys jumped from the taxi and lost themselves in the passing throng of pedestrians.

They had not gone far when Frank and Joe noticed that a tall man seemed to be trailing them. His face was almost hidden by the pulled-down brim of his felt hat. The Hardys were struck by something familiar about the fellow! But there was no time to mull this over.

"Better shake him," Frank muttered.

Joe agreed. Quickly the boys hailed a taxi and resumed their drive to the haulage company. When they arrived, the owner said:

"Ah, *sé*, I have the boxes all prepared. The covers, of course, will not be nailed down."

A few minutes later Chet and Tony joined them. The boys took their places in the big crates, which were loaded on to a truck. Soon they were bumping and rattling through the streets of San Juan.

When the truck arrived at the warehouse, the boxes were carried inside to the main room. As closing time neared, the workmen's voices died away and everything became quiet.

The first half hour of the boys' vigil went slowly. Cramped and tense in their hiding places, they sweated out each passing moment.

Then Frank heard a noise!

· 11 ·

Warehouse Marauders

FRANK strained his ears, wondering if he was mistaken. Then he heard it again—a faint scratchy noise which he could not identify.

Raising the lid of his box, he beamed a torch towards the queer sound. A large sheet of dirty wrapping paper lay a few yards away. On it crouched a small, brown, furry creature.

"What gives?" came a whisper from Joe's box.

"Just a rat."

The rodent froze for a few seconds in the glare of light, its beady eyes shining with reflected brilliance. Then it scampered off into a dark hole nearby—apparently the opening to a small tunnel for an electrical conduit, but large enough for a person to crawl into.

The boys resumed their wait, shifting occasionally to exercise their cramped muscles. The warehouse lay wrapped in gloom, pierced only by a faint glow from the moon through a skylight.

Some time later another noise broke the stillness. It was a faint curse in Spanish! The voice sounded oddly hollow and muffled.

Frank and Joe raised the lids of their crates a crack. A moment later they saw two figures wriggle through the tunnel opening. Both snapped on torches and played them around the room. Then the intruders, whose faces were in darkness, separated and began examining the shipping labels on the boxes and crates.

One of the men approached the spot where the Hardys were hiding. The boys closed the lids noiselessly and held their breaths. Through a knothole, Joe could make out one man's legs, scarcely inches away. Apparently he was examining the label on Joe's box!

A cold sweat broke out on the youth's forehead. *What if he opened the lid?*

"Hey, come here!" called out a raspy voice.

"*Qué quieres?*" said the man near Joe.

"Think I've found somethin' good—a box of fine Swiss watches! Should make a real haul!"

"Ah, *bueno!*"

As the Spanish-speaking intruder moved away, Joe gave a noiseless sigh of relief.

The boys could hear muttered conversation as the thieves discussed the loot. Cautiously Frank and Joe raised the lids of their boxes. A moment later Chet and Tony lifted theirs.

They could see the figures of the two burglars silhouetted by their own torches. They were squatting in front of a small crate, their backs to the boys. One of them seemed to be holding a bag.

Scarcely daring to breathe, the four boys watched tensely. One of the men produced a fine saw and began cutting deftly along the label of the box containing the watches.

In a few minutes an opening was made. The thief reached in and removed the packaged watches. Then his partner began filling the box with sand and rubble from the bag to equal its previous weight.

"Okay. Now!" hissed Frank, giving the signal to attack.

Moving silently, the four boys started to climb out of their crates. Chet was the first to emerge completely. But, in his eagerness, he let the crate lid slip from his sweaty fingers.

B-a-a-ang!

Instantly the burglars sprang to their feet. "Somebody's here!" cried one of them.

The other shrilled, "*Vamonos!* Let's go!"

Clicking off their flashlights, the two thieves darted off into the darkness. But the boys snapped on their own lights and managed to pin the fleeing men for a moment in the yellow beams.

One of the thieves was heavy-set, dark, and swarthy. The other, slim and blond, bore a startling resemblance to Joe!

The Hardys became tense with excitement. Was this the contact man of the gang—the one who had chloroformed Jack Wayne back at the Bayport airfield?

"I'll guard the tunnel," Frank told his brother. "The rest of you scatter!"

The two thieves had already taken cover among the barrels and crates.

"One of 'em's over there!" shouted Tony. But a crash of boxes indicated that their quarry was already plunging off.

Joe, Tony, and Chet lost no time in pursuing him. Soon the darkened warehouse was a scene of bedlam.

"I wonder where the watchman is," thought Frank. "He must have been knocked out."

Crates were banged over, piles of goods and boxes sent toppling as hunters and quarry blundered about in the darkness.

"Help! I've got him!" Chet panted, in a far corner of the warehouse.

Tony sprinted to aid him. His beam picked out the blond man, struggling in Chet's bearlike embrace. Instantly Tony tackled the fellow around the knees just as he jerked loose from Chet. The stout boy flashed his light square on the prisoner.

"It's the one who looks like Joe!" Chet cried out triumphantly.

"I *am* Joe!" howled the captive.

"Oh, *no!*" babbled Chet in nervous confusion.

Just then a yell from Frank brought the others whirling to attention. "They're getting away! Come quickly!"

The three boys raced in the direction of Frank's voice. But it was too late. During the mêlée between Chet, Joe, and Tony, the two suspects had grabbed Frank and pinned him behind a stack of barrels. Then they had wriggled through the tunnel.

"Come on! Let's go after them!" cried Joe.

He started to crawl into the tunnel headfirst, but Tony dragged him back.

"No, Joe. Don't try it! Those guys have the advantage."

"But we can't let 'em get away!" Joe protested in exasperation.

In the meantime, Chet had released Frank and they ran forward.

"Let's try the door!" Frank suggested. "Maybe we can nail the men when they come out the other end of the tunnel."

He led the way eagerly towards the door. The others hurried after him, and tried to push it open.

"Locked!" he cried.

The boys hurried to a door leading to the office and let themselves outside. Behind a bench an elderly man was groggily getting to his feet.

"You the watchman here?" Frank asked.

"*Sí.* I—I think—someone—knock me out."

"You're right. Two thieves who've just robbed this place. We're after them now. Where's the exit to the tunnel?"

The dazed watchman led the boys to the marauders' point of exit, an open manhole with its cover overturned. The discovery brought fresh groans.

"Of all the rotten breaks!" Joe grumbled.

Just then Frank heard the sound of a car starting up in the distance. "There they go!" he shouted, as twin headlights swept a path through the darkness.

Joe glanced around frantically for some way to take up the chase. He spotted a small motorcycle. "Whose is that?"

"It is mine, señor," the bewildered watchman admitted.

"May I borrow it?"

"*Sí, sí!* But be careful—*por favor!*"

Joe dashed towards the motorcycle, leaped into the saddle, and kicked the starter. The engine sputtered to life. With a blast of exhaust, he took off after the fleeing car.

The noise of the motorcycle gave warning to th
thieves that they were being followed. At top speed the
flashed through the darkened residential district
Santurce, then into the old town of San Juan.

For most of the way, Joe managed to keep the ca
clearly in view. But after passing San Cristóbal fortres
on the right, he emerged into the Plaza Colón to fin
that the burglars' car was no longer in sight.

In the centre of the square on a tall pillar, a bronz
statue of Christopher Columbus loomed against th
night sky.

"Oh, brother! If you could only talk!" Joe mutter
helplessly.

Obviously the thieves had disappeared down one
the narrow, cobblestoned streets leading off the squar
But which one?

Wheeling over to a parked taxi, Joe questioned th
driver about a speeding car. "Ah, *sí*, señor. It went tha
way!" replied the driver, pointing down one of th
streets.

"Thanks! *Muchas gracias!*" Joe exclaimed.

So that the warehouse thieves wouldn't hear hi
approaching, he parked the motorcycle near th
entrance to the narrow street and then continued c
foot. He had gone scarcely a hundred yards when
gasped jubilantly. Ahead in the moonlight stood th
thief who resembled Joe!

He was putting something into a basket which ha
been lowered by rope from a balcony. Joe had seen th
same method being used earlier that evening whe
people purchased fruit or vegetables from street vendor

Sprinting forward, Joe tried to take the man

surprise. Unfortunately, the fellow spotted him and darted into a narrow, twisting street.

Quickly Joe reached up and managed to grab the basket. But the man on the balcony gave it a hard yank, jerking it free. The basket shot up out of Joe's grasp.

The young sleuth tried to find an entrance to the building, but apparently there was none facing the street. He retraced his steps part of the way to the square and found an alley which led back to the houses. Cautiously he made his way through the shadowy, musty passageway.

Counting the buildings, Joe found the one from which the basket had been lowered. It was a two-storey building of pink stucco, with shuttered windows and a wrought-iron balcony on each of the two upper stories. An outside flight of steps led up to its gloomy-looking interior.

Joe started up the steps on tiptoe. But he did not get far. Suddenly he was struck on the head. Joe slumped to the ground, unconscious.

· 12 ·

The Tattooed Prisoner

BACK at the warehouse, Frank, Chet, and Tony waited anxiously for Joe to return. The police had come and gone. The boys had given the watchman first aid and he was now feeling better.

"Joe's been gone for almost an hour," muttered Frank, glancing worriedly at his watch.

"Why don't we get a taxi," Tony suggested, "and see if we can find him?"

"Second the motion!" Chet responded.

But finding a taxi at that hour was not easy and the boys finally had to go to the airport to get one. Since the thieves' car had sped away in the direction of Santurce, Frank ordered the driver to try that part of the city first. But fifteen minutes of cruising up and down the darkened streets proved fruitless.

"Take us into Old San Juan," Frank said.

As they drove into Columbus Plaza, Chet exclaimed, "There's the motorcycle Joe borrowed!"

It was standing parked at the kerb where Joe had left it, but the young sleuth was nowhere in sight. Frank paid their driver, and gave him an extra dollar to take the motorcycle back to the watchman at once.

The three boys began a search of the surrounding

streets for Joe. But the hunt was unsuccessful and finally they gave up in despair.

"Guess we may as well go back to the hotel," Frank said glumly. "But I sure hate to tell Dad that Joe's missing."

Mr Hardy was greatly dismayed by the news. "With the gang we're up against, anything may have happened to Joe!" he declared.

Before he could formulate a plan of action, there was a knock on the door of the hotel room.

"You are Señor Fenton Hardy?" a Puerto Rican police officer asked.

"That's right."

"You have a son named Joe Hardy?"

"I certainly do. You have news of him?" Mr Hardy asked anxiously.

"I regret to inform you, señor, that your son is in jail."

The officer, expecting to hear alarmed protests from the group, was amazed to see looks of relief on their faces.

"We'll go to see him at once," Mr Hardy told the officer.

A police car took them to San Juan Police Headquarters. Here they learned, to their amazement, that Joe was being held for attempted burglary. A warden took them to his dimly lit cell.

"There he is, señor," said the jailer.

The blond figure inside was slumped dejectedly on his cot, a livid bruise on one temple. But at sight of Mr Hardy and the others, he brightened and jumped to his feet.

"Am I glad to see *you* people!"

Mr Hardy was about to greet his son when Chet cried out in alarm. "Look! It's not Joe! It's that fellow who resembles him!"

Chet pointed out that on the prisoner's left forearm was a pineapple tattoo! To everybody's surprise, the prisoner merely laughed.

"Had you fooled, Chet," he said. "It's only a joke. I put the pineapple on myself with this indelible pencil I borrowed from the guard."

Frank chuckled with relief. "You're Joe, all right. Someday that stunt may come in handy."

"Now that you have been identified," said Mr Hardy, "suppose you tell us why you're here."

Joe told about the basket incident and how he had tried to enter the house by a rear stair. "Someone conked me. When I came to, the guy claimed I was a burglar and called the police!"

"Hmm." Mr Hardy regarded his son with a wry smile. "I suppose you can hardly blame the fellow for being suspicious."

"That's if he's on the level," said Joe. "But I have a hunch he was more interested in keeping me from finding out what was in the basket!"

"We'll check up on the place," Mr Hardy said.

After showing his credentials, the detective obtained Joe's release. Although the officer in charge was a bit dubious, he issued a search warrant and dispatched a police car to take the group to the house in question.

They climbed the stairs to the rear entrance and knocked. A thin old man opened the door.

The policeman said in Spanish that they had a warrant to search the house for stolen goods.

The old man seemed bewildered, but allowed them to enter. He informed them that a separate family lived on each floor. Mr Hardy and the policeman questioned all the occupants and searched every room with the help of the boys. Nothing suspicious was found and the man who had charged Joe with burglary was not at home.

"Looks like a wild-goose chase," Chet murmured as the searchers reached the top floor.

Frank, too, was about ready to give up when he caught sight of a small white card on the floor. He took out his handkerchief, wiped some dust off his hands, then dropped the handkerchief on the floor as if accidentally. He picked it up casually and returned the handkerchief to his pocket. A few minutes later the group left.

When they gathered later in Mr Hardy's hotel room, the private investigator tossed his Panama hat on the bed with a sigh.

"Well, boys, it was a good try," he told them, "but we seem to have run into a blind alley."

Frank grinned. "Maybe not, Dad."

He pulled out the handkerchief and extracted the small white card. "I found this on the top floor," he explained, "but I didn't want to mention it in front of the people who lived there."

Mr Hardy and the others read the card in amazement. It bore the words, crudely printed by hand:

CABEZONA N

Joe whistled loudly. "It's the same code message we worked out from those dummy instructions back in

Bayport!" he exclaimed. "This house may be a hideout for the gang!"

"You're probably right, son," said his father, furrowing his brow. "But we may have a hard time convincing the police of that."

He and the boys discussed the mystery for nearly an hour before retiring, but arrived at no solution. The next morning they breakfasted together in the pleasant hotel dining room.

"Mmm, boy, this iced pineapple juice is good!" Chet smacked his lips.

Just then a bellboy came to their table. He informed Mr Hardy that a visitor was waiting in the foyer. The detective asked to be excused and left. When he returned, there was a grave expression on his face.

"Who was it, Dad?" Frank asked.

"A United States federal agent," Mr Hardy replied quietly. "Something new and serious has come up on my case. I'm not free to tell you any more just now, but it looks as though you boys will have to carry on here by yourselves."

Frank, Joe, Chet and Tony enthusiastically said they were ready. Mr Hardy informed them that he and Jack Wayne would have to take off at once for a secret destination. He quickly finished his meal and said goodbye.

After breakfast the four boys assembled in Frank and Joe's room.

"It seems to me," said Joe, "that the house we searched last night is still our best lead. I think we ought to watch it."

"Check and double check," Tony said.

Frank agreed but said that to avoid suspicion they should not all take on the job at once. "We'd surely be spotted. Tony, how about you taking the first watch? With your olive complexion, you could pass for a native."

Tony grinned. "That's fine with me." He promptly left by taxi for Columbus Plaza.

The other three boys decided to look through the telephone directory on the off-chance that "Cabezona" might be a person's name. Chet offered to check on this.

"Only one person in the whole city of San Juan named Cabezona," he informed the others after he ran his finger down the page. "And his initials are F. X.— not N."

"Let's talk to him, anyway," urged Joe.

The boys left the hotel and asked the doorman for directions to the Avenida Ponce de Leon. At the address Chet had jotted down was a haberdashery shop. The owner, Señor F. X. Cabezona, was a stout, jolly man who spoke excellent English.

"And what may I show the young men? Shirts? Socks?" He beamed at his three customers.

"A tie, please," Frank replied.

The proprietor showed them an assortment of gay ties, then said there were some that they might like in a new shipment just unpacked. He disappeared into a back room.

While he was gone, Chet whispered, "This can't be the right Cabezona."

"He sure doesn't dook like a racketeer," Joe agreed.

When the owner returned, Frank said casually, "Your name is rather unusual."

"Ah, *sí!*" The jolly man chuckled. "In Puerto Rico the word means the big pineapples which grow on the south coast."

Pineapples! The Hardys and Chet were elated. They had picked up another clue! Maybe the word in the Hugo instructions and on the card Frank had found referred to the pineapple tattoo! It must be the gang's identification!

The affable shopkeeper went on, "So far as I know, my wife and young son Carlos and I are the only Cabezona family on the island."

Frank and Joe wondered if there could be another Cabezona in Puerto Rico, perhaps living there secretly and leading the underground group.

After buying a tie, the boys returned to their hotel. When they reached their room, the phone was ringing. Joe answered. It was Tony calling.

"I just saw a tall guy with a large head sneak into the alley behind the house. How about you fellows getting over here? I have a hunch something's up!"

"We're on our way!" Joe promised. "Meet you at the statue of Columbus."

He put down the phone and relayed the news to Frank and Chet. Both were jubilant.

"That man might be the one who trailed us on our way to the haulage company last night," Joe pointed out.

"Not only that," said Frank, "but maybe his nickname is Cabezona!"

· 13 ·

Pursuit at El Morro

WHEN the Hardys and Chet reached Columbus Plaza in a taxi, they saw Tony standing in the doorway of a small souvenir shop. It was on the corner of the narrow street to which Joe had traced the mystery man.

"Okay, right here, driver!" said Frank. The passengers got out and Tony came over to join them.

"Now tell us everything, Tony," Joe requested when the group walked on a little, out of anyone else's hearing.

"Well, first of all, I want to tell you I've hired a swell observation post for us. Cost a buck," Tony explained. "It's a room in a house right across the street from the hideout. We'll have a clear view of both the pink stucco place and the alley."

"Good work!" said Joe.

The boys hurried down the narrow, cobblestoned street, then ducked into the side entrance of the house where Tony had rented a room. They posted themselves at the front windows of the room. Latticed shutters enabled them to peer out without being seen. Almost an hour went by without results.

"You sure you weren't seeing things?" complained Chet, who was feeling warm.

"Positive!" said Tony. "Give the man in there a chance. If he went in, he's bound to come out *sometime*!"

"Unless we've already missed him," Chet retorted.

The words were hardly out of his mouth when Tony exclaimed in a low voice, "There he is!"

A tall man, with an unusually large head, emerged from the alley. He was swarthy and had an aquiline-shaped nose.

"Abdul!" Frank exclaimed excitedly. "*He's* the fellow who was shadowing us, Joe."

His brother nodded. "We couldn't place him then with that hat over his face, plus not wearing his fancy Oriental getup."

The assistant to Hugo the fortune teller, hatless now, wore dungarees and a striped jersey.

"There *is* a connection between those Hugo-dummy smugglers and the freight thieves!" said Frank.

"Let's follow him!" Joe urged.

The four started out at once, keeping a safe distance behind the man. Abdul headed away from Columbus Plaza. At Calle San Justo he turned right and walked for several blocks, then walked to the left on the Boulevard del Valle.

Eventually he came to a broad iron gate standing open to visitors. It was the entrance to Fort Brooke, the big United States military post at the western tip of Old San Juan. With a casual salute to the soldier on guard, Abdul strolled on through.

"Gallopin' gooseberries!" Chet burst out. "What's he up to now? Is he going to steal some military secrets?"

"Only one way to find out," Frank replied, hurrying towards the fort.

As the boys passed through the gate, a grassy green plateau stretched ahead of them. It swept out towards the ocean and was used as a golf course. Men and women were playing golf. Tourists' cars stood parked along the road, which curved to the left of the course. Facing this was a row of Army buildings and officers' homes.

"Let's separate and act like sightseers," Frank advised his companions.

Each of them started wandering round alone, but kept a wary eye on Abdul. The man headed straight for the old Spanish battlements of El Morro. This ancient fort stood poised on a bluff jutting out over the sea, beyond the end of the golf course.

When Abdul reached the massive stone walls of the fortress, he glanced around for a moment. Seemingly satisfied that no one was following him, he ducked hastily into a round, stone sentry house at the very tip of the rock-walled point. Below it, the surf pounded itself into foam over the coral rocks.

"Now why did he do that?" Chet asked himself, puzzled.

The boys began closing in. Frank reached the spot first and made his way along the wall of the steep parapet where an ancient bronze cannon offered a convenient hiding place. Frank crouched down behind it to watch Abdul.

Inside the sentry box the man took a mirror from his pocket and aimed it to catch the sun. Then he began shooting flashes of light out to sea. Frank had a clear view.

"He's signalling in international code!" the boy realized with a gasp of excitement.

Slowly the message was spelled out: "3–4–8–9–P–M–Skeleton."

Frank wondered what it meant and who was receiving the message. He stood up and glanced across the water. Half a mile out he could see a blue speedboat.

Just then Abdul turned to leave the sentry house. With a start he noticed Frank standing behind the cannon. At the same moment, the other three boys burst from their hiding places.

Muttering a threat, Abdul took off like a bolt of lightning, heading for the road. Joe tried to nail him with a flying tackle, but the huge man swept the boy aside with a single blow of his great arm.

"Stop him!" yelled Frank to a soldier and several sightseers. "He's wanted by the police!"

Most of the tourists were bewildered by the sudden commotion, but some of the onlookers grabbed for the fugitive too late. Startled golfers watched the chase wonderingly.

By this time, Abdul was streaking across the links with the boys in hot pursuit. Despite his weight, the man covered the ground with amazing speed. Even Joe and Frank, who were top runners at Bayport High, could not catch up with him.

Abdul reached the road just as a delivery truck passed. He leaped on to the tailboard, and in a matter of seconds, the vehicle rumbled through the gate.

"He's getting away!" Joe shouted, clenching his fists in bitter disappointment.

At that moment one of the golfers rushed forward.

"Jump into my car!" he cried, sprinting towards a white convertible.

Panting their thanks, Frank and Joe piled in with him. As the car shot forward, the boys poured out their story in bits and snatches.

"That fellow's wanted by the police," Frank explained. "He's part of a smuggling ring."

"I hope we can catch him," the driver said.

Fortunately, due to the town's narrow streets, traffic had to move slowly. Swinging down Calle Cristo, they soon caught sight of the delivery truck. It had turned left into Calle Sol only to find the way blocked by a pushcart pedlar.

"This'll do!" Joe said to their driver. "A million thanks."

The boys leaped from the car and ran towards the truck, Joe in the lead. To his dismay, Abdul was no longer aboard!

"Pardon me," Joe said to the man at the wheel. "Where's the big fellow who hitched a ride with you?"

The driver leaned out of his cab and pointed down the street. "He jumped off the truck and went into that restaurant, señor! *Caramba!* What kind of game is going on here?"

Without waiting to explain, the boys dashed off. A moment later they pulled up to a sliding halt as Joe caught sight of the restaurant's name.

"Look!" he gasped. "*El Calypso Caliente*—Hot Calypso! It's the password used at the airport back in Eastern City!"

"Hold it a second," Frank cautioned as his brother started inside. "Tony, you and Chet wait outside in case Abdul tries another fast one. If you see him come out, grab him."

"Right!"

Frank and Joe entered the restaurant and glanced round swiftly. Abdul was not in sight, so they headed towards the back of the place.

The white-jacketed proprietor bustled forward to bar the way. He was a rather sinister-looking man with a heavy beard.

"You wish something to eat, señores?"

"We're looking for a man who's wanted by the police," Frank told him. "He came in here a few minutes ago."

"What did he look like?"

"A big fellow in a striped jersey."

The proprietor bared his teeth in a wide smile. "You are wrong, señores. No one of that description has entered the restaurant."

"Suppose we look in the kitchen, just in case," Frank suggested.

The owner hesitated, then raised his voice slightly and said in Spanish, "Visitors coming to the kitchen." To the boys he added, "*Muy bien*, señores. You may go in, if you wish."

He gestured towards the swinging doors that led to the kitchen.

"Thanks," Frank said crisply and strode forward, ahead of Joe.

But as Frank pushed the doors open, his face suddenly blanched in alarm.

· 14 ·

The Unseen Enemy

"Look out, Joe!" Frank yelled as he ducked to the floor of the restaurant's kitchen.

A sheet of boiling water flew at the boys, just as Joe dropped to his knees. Both boys barely avoided being scalded, as the water passed harmlessly over their heads.

The burly cook who had thrown the water stood holding a huge empty kettle in both hands. Joe was white-faced with anger. He jumped to his feet, ready to fly at the man with both fists.

"Why, you big—!" he exploded.

Frank interrupted with a shout, "Look! There goes Abdul!"

The man was darting out the back door. Frank and Joe started after him, but the stout chef blocked their way, saying, "Ah, I am so sorry about the water, *amigos!*"

He stepped back with a look of dismay as he spied the tattoo of indelible pencil still visible on Joe's arm.

"Please, Beppo!" he trembled. "I did not mean to—"

"Shut up, you fool!" the proprietor snarled.

The chef's words ended in a gulp, but he kept on staring at Joe with a strange look.

"Who's Beppo?" Frank demanded.

The cook said nothing, pretending not to understand.

"Maybe he's my double," said Joe.

Once more the owner assumed his pleasant expression. "He is confused, señor. I fear this little accident has greatly upset him. And now if you will kindly leave—"

"Not yet!" snapped Frank. "You two are mixed up in some kind of racket and we intend to find out what it's all about. If you don't want to tell us, maybe you'd rather talk to the police."

"The police!" Obviously dismayed by Frank's threat, the proprietor suddenly became nervously polite.

"I will tell you everything. That big man—he rushed in here and said he wanted to hide. And if we told someone called Beppo, who has a pineapple tattoo, or anyone else that he was here, he would kill us. So I gave you a lie. I am so sorry."

"But what about that hot water?" Joe asked.

The cook spoke up. "The big man made me throw it. He held me at gunpoint—otherwise I would not do such a terrible thing!"

Frank and Joe did not know whether to believe the story, but they could not refute it. Finally Frank said, "Okay. We'll go now."

Both the cook and the proprietor looked relieved.

Outside, Tony and Chet were waiting eagerly. The Hardys related what had happened.

"You fellows should have crowned 'em both with that empty kettle!" Chet exploded indignantly.

"What now?" said Tony. "Go to the police?"

Frank shook his head. "Those men in there just *might* be telling the truth. Anyhow, we have plenty of other leads to keep us busy."

"How about that motorboat Abdul might have been signalling from El Morro?" Joe asked.

"I'd say it was worth checking up on. With that blue colour, it should be easy to spot, if it's still in this area."

"Let me handle that end of it," Tony suggested. "I'm really aching for a chance to do some power-cruising in these waters!"

Back in Bayport, Tony owned a boat called the *Napoli II*, in which he spent most of his spare time.

The boys took a taxi to the oceanfront. It was a beautiful day and the sea sparkled in the sunshine. The four sleuths ate lunch at a restaurant specializing in seafood, then Frank hired a trim little speedboat.

"Oh, boy, I can hardly wait to take her out!" Tony gloated as he warmed up the motor.

"We should stick in pairs to be on the safe side," Joe said thoughtfully. Chet offered to accompany Tony.

A few moments later the two boys *put-putted* out across the water. Frank and Joe returned to the hotel, eager to work further on the clue of the pineapple tattoo, and, if possible, to link it with the word *Cabezona*. While there Joe scrubbed the indelible mark from his arm.

"Let's talk to the hotel manager," Frank suggested. They found him in his office and engaged him in conversation.

"Does the word *Cabezona* mean anything to you?" Frank inquired.

"It means a large head," the manager responded. He looked at the boys quizzically. "Why do you ask?"

"Is Cabezona ever used to mean a pineapple?" Joe questioned.

The manager scratched his head in thought for a moment. "I don't know," he said. "But I suppose the word could be used when referring to a large pineapple. If you are interested in pineapples, a friend of mine could give you information on the subject. He is Juan Delgado and owns a pineapple plantation at Manati."

"We'd sure appreciate it if you could arrange for us to pay a visit," said Frank.

"I will call him at once."

The manager put through the call and carried on a rapid, pleasant conversation in Spanish. When he hung up, he turned to the boys with a smile.

"It is all arranged. He will expect you early this afternoon."

"Thank you," said Frank. "You've been a great help."

The brothers went to a car-hire agency, and made arrangements for hiring a convertible.

The attendant provided them with a road map of the island, saying, "Just follow the directions I have marked, señores."

The drive was thoroughly enjoyable, with a cool trade wind steadily blowing in from the sea. On their left, the blue-green mountains rose towards the cloudless sky.

The lush coastal plain was dotted with waving seas of sugar cane, interspersed here and there with fields of pineapple planted in orderly rows.

In places the road became hilly, with shade trees

arching overhead. Some were *flamboyantes*, the flame trees with gorgeous red blossoms.

"Things really grow here!" Joe said admiringly.

"Like living in a flower garden!" Frank remarked. "Mother and Aunt Gertrude would love this."

Arriving in Manati, the boys inquired the way to the Delgado plantation and were told it was situated one mile north of town. When they reached it, Señor Delgado greeted them cordially on the steps of his long, low, white bungalow.

"Welcome, *amigos!* I understand you have come to learn about pineapples."

"Yes, Señor Delgado," Frank said as he and Joe shook hands with the man. "Cabezona pineapples."

The plantation owner drove the boys round, pointing out the fields of spiked plants in various stages of growth. Men were busy in one section cutting off huge pineapples with long, sharp knives. Then, after showing Frank and Joe the huge cannery, he took them into his office. A white-jacketed Puerto Rican boy brought glasses and a pitcher of iced pineapple juice on a tray.

"And now, perhaps you would like to ask me some questions," said Señor Delgado as they all sipped the fruit juice.

Shooting a quick glance at his brother, Frank decided to take the plantation owner into their confidence. When the servant left, he explained that they were trying to solve a mystery.

"We have an idea," Frank said, "that a certain dangerous group in Puerto Rico may use a pineapple as a sort of insignia. Have you ever heard of anyone wearing a pineapple tattoo on his left forearm?"

Señor Delgado shook his head. "I have never heard of such a thing, señores, but it is certainly possible."

Joe inquired if Cabezona were the name of a place somewhere in Puerto Rico. Again Señor Delgado replied in the negative.

But the native servant, returning just in time to hear the question, interrupted politely, "Excuse me, señores, but I have heard of a small place called Punta Cabezona on the coast north of here. The people call it this because the land is thickly overgrown, and looks like a huge pineapple. It is near the La Palma sugar *central*."

"Sugar *central*?" Joe repeated as both boys tried hard to conceal their excitement.

"A mill where the sugar cane is ground up and crushed," Señor Delgado explained. "I have never heard of this Punta Cabezona, but I can at least give you a note of introduction to the owner of the *central*, and he can give you exact directions."

He quickly wrote the note, then the boys drove off. Some time later the mill came into view, in the midst of vast fields of sugar cane. A tall stack, jutting up from the mill's corrugated iron roof, belched a steady plume of smoke.

"The whole air smells sweet around here," Joe observed.

Frank stopped the car and they got out at a small building with a sign marked *Office*. Inside, they found the manager and gave him Señor Delgado's note. After reading it, the man rubbed his chin and looked puzzled.

"I am sorry, but I myself am new in this district. However, I am sure that my foreman, Rodriguez, could direct you to this Punta Cabezona. You will find him working the cane crusher in the mill."

The boys walked over to the main *central* building. Trucks and tractor-trains loaded with cane were drawn up outside. Huge cranes lifted the stalks and dumped them into a chute.

Frank and Joe entered and found themselves in a dark bedlam of noise. Giant rollers ground the cane into juice, which was then pumped into hot, spinning kettles to be granulated into sugar.

A flight of steel steps led up to a narrow catwalk. At the far end was an enclosed cab, where the operator controlled the crushers.

"That must be Rodriguez up there." Frank had to shout to make himself heard.

The boys climbed the stairs and made their way along the catwalk, clinging to a slender handrail. They were fascinated by the scene below. On their left were the huge rollers. On the right there was a steep drop past the giant flywheel into a pit of churning machinery.

Suddenly Frank and Joe were shoved from behind. Taken off guard, they lost their balance. With wild yells, the boys toppled over the left-hand rail!

· 15 ·

Atomic Cargo

As FRANK went over the railing, he managed to clutch an iron upright with one hand. Joe grabbed his brother's belt. White with fear, the two boys hung dangling above the pit of sugar-crushing machinery!

"Help! Help!" they shouted. But the thundering machinery drowned out their voices.

Would Senor Rodriguez hear their cries in time to save them from a horrible fate?

Joe reached up, and by stretching was able to grasp a bar and let go the belt. The boys' last ounce of strength was ebbing fast when Frank saw a figure in tan work clothes running along the catwalk towards them.

"Hang on, Joe!" he gasped. "Someone's coming!"

An instant later Frank's wrist was seized in a strong grip, while another brawny arm reached down to grab Joe's. Singlehanded, the foreman hauled the boys across the rail.

By the time the Hardys were dropping weakly on to the catwalk, two other workmen arrived on the scene to lend a hand.

"*Santa Maria!*" gasped the boys' rescuer, who had turned pale himself. "Never have I seen such a narrow escape!"

The men helped Frank and Joe down the iron steps and out into the fresh air.

"Thank you. Thank you very much," Frank said to the man who had saved their lives. "Are you Señor Rodriguez?"

"*Sí*, I am Rodriguez," the foreman replied. "And now do you mind telling me the reason why you came so close to killing yourselves?"

Joe explained what had happened, adding that the boys had not seen the person who had shoved them. The brawny foreman exploded with anger. "If I get my hands on that killer, I will wring his neck!"

Turning to the workers, he asked in Spanish if any of them had witnessed the incident. One man told of having seen a man run down from the catwalk and flee out the door. Through the mill window, he had seen him drive off in a car.

Rodriguez said to the boys, "I can assure you none of my men would try such a hideous trick!"

"I believe you," Frank said quietly, then after a pause, he asked, "We came here to get directions to a place called Punta Cabezona."

"Ah, *sí*," said Rodriguez. "It is about five or six miles from here, but the road there is rather rough." He gave the boys careful directions, and expressed the hope they would meet again under pleasanter circumstances.

Frank and Joe thanked him, then walked back to the *central* office. As they entered, the manager looked up.

"Did your friend find you, señores?" he inquired.

"What friend?" Joe asked in surprise.

"I did not catch his name, but he was a very tall man

with a large head. I told him you had just gone over to the mill."

Frank and Joe exchanged knowing glances. *Abdul!* But how did he know they were here?

After telling briefly about their close brush with death, Frank asked if he might use the telephone to call Señor Delgado. The manager, distressed that he had unwittingly helped the would-be killer, hastily agreed.

"I—I do not know what to say, señores!" he gasped.

"It wasn't your fault," Frank assured him.

The manager helped to put through the call, and Frank spoke to Señor Delgado.

"This is Frank Hardy," he told the plantation owner. "Did anyone come there looking for us after we left?"

Joe saw his brother's face tighten as he listened to the reply. When he hung up, Frank's eyes were grim.

"Well, that explains it," he said. "Abdul must have trailed us to the pineapple plantation. He arrived there right after we left and said he had an urgent message for us. So of course Señor Delgado told him where we'd gone."

"He must be a bad enemy," the manager commented.

"We agree," the Hardys chorused.

Realizing that they were still in grave danger, the Hardys drove cautiously to Punta Cabezona. The dirt road twisted through palm groves and canopies of dense green vegetation. When the boys arrived, Frank stopped the car and they got out.

"Easy to see how this place got its name," he remarked, peering ahead.

The spit of land, jutting out to sea, ended in a bulging mound. This was topped with bushy green foliage, which sprouted outwards from the crown of the hill, giving the place the appearance of a huge pineapple.

"But I wonder how it ties in with the gang," Joe said with a puzzled frown. "The place appears to be deserted."

The boys strolled out on to the tiny peninsula, and climbed the hill. Reaching the top, they poked about among the bushes and vegetation. But the thick underbrush showed no sign of having been trampled by human feet!

The Hardys were baffled. "I was sure we were on to something," Frank said, disappointed. "Let's walk along the shore."

They encountered several natives on the way. When questioned, none of them could recall having seen anybody lurking around the point.

"Why should a person go out there, señor?" said one old man in Spanish, shrugging his shoulders. "Without a machete to chop down brush, there is hardly even a place to sit down!"

A few moments later a plane droned overhead. Frank looked up and noted that it was flying due north. Suddenly he snapped his fingers.

"Cabezona N!" he whispered excitedly. "Say, Joe, that N might be a directional signal, meaning north of here. Maybe it leads to the gang's hideout!"

"In the middle of the ocean?" Joe questioned dubiously.

"No! It could be some island north of Puerto Rico!" Frank explained.

Joe was impressed by his brother's theory. "Maybe you've hit it," he admitted. "Well, locating it will be our next trip, I suppose."

Elated over the clue, the boys returned to San Juan. By the time they reached the hotel, it was seven o'clock. Tony and Chet had not returned yet.

"They must be doing some real sleuthing," Frank commented, a little worried.

The Hardys waited a while, but finally went down to the hotel dining room. Frank and Joe, growing anxious about their friends, had little appetite for their meal. As they forced themselves to eat, they discussed the message which Abdul had flashed out to sea: "3-4-8-9-P-M-Skeleton."

"That 'PM' part sounds like a time signal to me," Joe remarked.

"Sure, but a signal for what?"

Joe mulled over the problem. "Well, this is a shot in the dark," he admitted, "but how about a rendezvous at the airport? After all, if the racket we're investigating is the theft of air-freight shipments, there might be some flight coming in that the gang is watching for."

Frank nodded. "That makes sense."

After finishing their supper, the two boys sat in the foyer and waited another half hour for Chet and Tony, but they failed to appear.

"I think I'll phone the police," Frank said.

He put in a call and asked if any boat had been reported in trouble. The answer was No.

"That's a relief," Frank told Joe. "But I'd feel better if Chet and Tony were here."

"I'm getting the creeps waiting," said Joe. "Suppose

ve go out to the airport to investigate cargo flights."

"Okay."

After leaving a message for their friends, they took a taxi to the field. On the schedule board inside the air-freight operations office all incoming flights were listed.

Frank gave a gasp. "You hit the nail on the head, Joe!" he exclaimed. "Look there!"

According to the board, cargo flight No. 348, en route from New York to South America, would stop at the field at 9 p.m.

Joe glanced at his watch. "Almost that now. Let's go out and take a look."

The boys strolled up and down. Soon the green and red lights of a plane came into view overhead. Moments later, a large cargo ship thundered down out of the sky and taxied to a halt.

The boys moved closer, acting like casual sightseers. They watched as an unloading ramp was wheeled out to the plane and the crew disembarked.

"No one seems to be meeting any of them," Frank remarked. "That must mean that the message I picked up refers to the cargo." He added excitedly, "Maybe it's on the plane and the gang is planning to steal it!"

Joe nodded. "Keep your eyes on things. I'll try to contact the airport manager, or a guard."

"Roger!"

Left to himself, Frank strolled as close to the plane as he felt was safe, without attracting attention. Just then the pilot and co-pilot walked past him, heading for the flight operations office.

"I'll be glad when the run is over," Frank heard the

pilot say. "I don't like carrying this kind of top-secret cargo."

"No," said the co-pilot. "But at least it's well locked up."

Frank wondered if the pilot could mean component parts for atomic weapons. At that moment, out of the corner of his eye, Frank noticed two men who seemed to be watching the plane closely. They were standing perfectly still in the shadow of the cargo warehouse, which extended from the rear of the terminal building.

"I wonder who they are," Frank thought. "Probably detectives!"

At that moment two cargo handlers drove a forklift to the cargo compartment door which stood open. After removing several crates and boxes, they went off, leaving the door wide open.

Frank looked for the men in the shadows. They were gone!

"Could they have been security guards assigned to watch the plane," Frank reasoned, "or were they freight thieves?"

Frank wondered, too, if the handlers might have been bribed by the thieves not to close the cargo door! There might be a robbery of the plane's top-secret cargo at any moment!

With no help in sight, Frank decided on a bold move. He hurried towards the plane and climbed into the cargo hold, reasoning that his presence alone might baulk an attempted robbery. On the other hand, if the thief tried force, Frank could put up a fight and perhaps pin the man down until Joe arrived with the airport guards.

In the front of the cargo hatch was a metal-gated section, enclosing large steel-strapped boxes. Frank found the gate open and went forward to inspect the cargo.

Flicking on his pocket flashlight, he played the beam over the crates and boxes. Suddenly Frank was startled by a sound behind him. Looking up, he saw Joe a few feet away. In relief he said:

"I thought you'd gone for help. If those thieves are getting ready to rob this—"

Frank got no further. Too late he realized that the person was not Joe, but the smuggler who looked like him! The fellow's fist shot out, caught Frank on the jaw, and sent him sprawling.

Just before the young sleuth blacked out, he heard the door slam shut.

Frank was a prisoner!

Island of Danger

INSIDE the cargo compartment Frank slowly revived. When he realized the plane was airborne, he was seized with terror. The ship was soaring higher and higher and the cargo hold was not pressurized! Frank shuddered at the thought of blacking out for an indefinite time through lack of enough oxygen at high altitudes. Also, there was the danger of freezing to death!

At the airport, meanwhile, Joe had managed to locate the night manager, a husky balding man named Mr Lopez. Though somewhat doubtful about the boy's story, he promised to alert both the tower and the airport detectives for any sign of a disturbance. Joe returned to the field just in time to see the cargo plane take off. Apparently there had been no trouble.

Frank was nowhere in sight. Joe walked through the waiting room, looking up and down.

Suddenly an alarming thought struck Joe. Was Frank, by any chance, in the plane? Joe hurried back to the manager's office. Hastily he reported his brother's disappearance.

"Please call the plane back, Mr Lopez!" he exclaimed. "I'm sure Frank's locked in the cargo compartment."

The man looked puzzled. "Why you told me yourself

your brother had climbed out of the plane and reported everything was all right."

"*What?*"

"Look! Are you playing a game?" snapped Mr Lopez.

Joe turned pale. "I haven't been back here in your office since I first talked to you."

Breathlessly Joe explained how a man they thought was a smuggler was practically his double. "That faker has already posed as me once!" Joe went on. "He did it so he could sabotage our plane before we flew here. Now he's done it again, so they could trap my brother! Mr Lopez, you must bring that plane back!"

Though startled by what Joe had told him, Lopez hesitated.

"I can't bring back the plane just on your say-so," he protested. "Maybe your brother is still here. I'll have him paged on the loudspeaker."

In a moment the public-address system was blaring out Frank's name, asking him to call the manager's office at once. There was no response, but suddenly a startling bit of news was relayed to Lopez. The two detectives assigned to watch the cargo plane had been found unconscious.

Mr Lopez needed no further convincing about Frank's plight. He called the tower. "Radio Flight 348 to return to San Juan immediately. Emergency."

Up in the control tower, the operator barked the orders into his mike. Then he added, "Attention, all planes. An emergency landing is expected. All other ships in the air, circle the field until further notice. Repeat—circle the field."

An ambulance with oxygen equipment was rushed out on the field. Joe found the tension almost unbearable as he waited. At last the green and red lights of the cargo craft were sighted. A few minutes later the big plane landed and taxied down the runway.

Even before the landing wheels slowed to a halt, the ambulance roared out to meet it. Doctor, stretcher-bearers, and ground crew stood ready as the door of the cargo hatch was unlocked.

Joe, forced to watch from the apron, saw a still figure being carried out on to the stretcher. *Frank!* Breaking away from the manager and guards, Joe raced out on the field.

"Frank! Frank!" he cried frantically.

"Take it easy, son," said one of the ground crewmen, restraining him gently. "Doc's doing everything he can."

The stretcher was lifted into the ambulance and Joe jumped in after it. The doctor applied an oxygen mask to Frank, then he filled a hypodermic syringe and injected a stimulant.

Badly shaken, Joe could only watch and hope. After what seemed hours, he saw the colour seeping back into his brother's cheeks. Soon Frank became conscious, but he appeared dazed.

Joe flashed an anxious look at the doctor, who nodded reassuringly. "He's all right now. But it was a mighty close call! Fortunately for him the plane had not remained at high altitude for too long."

A few minutes later Frank, with a rueful grin, told his story. "I sure am glad the plane was called back," he remarked.

"Thank your brother," said the physician. "Now, young man, I want you to rest in our infirmary for an hour."

While Frank relaxed on a hospital bed, word came that there had been no theft of freight from the plane, but the two cargo handlers had admitted accepting money from some man to leave the cargo door open.

"I have a hunch you foiled a robbery," Joe told Frank. "That shipment of parts for an atomic weapon will reach its destination now."

"I hope so. But we didn't capture any of the gang. What's more, they'll probably make it tougher than ever for us."

Joe nodded in agreement.

When the doctor discharged Frank, the boys started back to their hotel. "I sure hope Chet and Tony are there," said Joe.

To their relief, the Hardys found that their two friends had just returned. They were sweaty and dishevelled. Tony had a cut on his forehead and Chet was hobbling on one leg.

"It looks as if you ran into trouble," Joe remarked in alarm.

"Real trouble," Chet confessed.

He said that after an hour of cruising, he and Tony had spotted the suspicious blue speedboat and given chase. Suddenly, though the blue craft was outrunning their own, it had turned round and deliberately bumped Tony's boat!

"As they went by," Tony took up the story, "the men in the boat hid their faces."

"You mean you didn't get a look at them?" Joe asked.

"Not a peek," Tony replied. "And, boy, did they really let us have it!"

The collision had dented the side of Tony's boat and disabled the propeller. Both Chet and Tony had been hurled from their seats and almost swept overboard by the speedboat's powerful wake.

"We managed to signal the harbour police by waving our shirts," Chet said. "They towed us into shore, then went to hunt for the blue boat."

"Any luck?" asked Frank.

"Not a bit," Chet replied. "We hung around the dock waiting for word till it got dark, but the police couldn't find any trace of the blue speedboat."

"I'll bet I know why," Joe said grimly. "Instead of coming back to port, those men made for an island offshore. That's probably the reason they smashed up Tony's boat—so you couldn't find out which way they were heading."

For the first time the four friends grinned and Frank said, "But they didn't fool us. Tomorrow we'll get another boat and head north of Cabezona."

"And now," said Tony, "tell Chet and me what you fellows have been doing."

When they heard the Hardys' story, their grins faded, and Chet said woefully, "All I wanted was a ventriloquist's dummy and look what happened!"

After another hour of conversation the four boys went to bed. The next morning they felt none the worse for their previous day's experiences. After a hearty breakfast of bacon and eggs, they took a taxi to the boat dock.

"Wonder how much that man'll charge us for damages," Tony said uncomfortably.

The boat owner, however, was quite cordial. "Do not worry, señores," he assured the boys. "The police have told me the whole story, and I know it was not your fault. Besides, the boat was covered by insurance."

This time, Frank hired a much faster speedboat and filled the tank with enough fuel for a long run. Heading westwards, they cruised along the Puerto Rican coast until Frank sighted a pineapple-shaped hill at the tip of a small spit of land.

"There's Punta Cabezona," he told Tony. "Now steer a course due north."

As they headed out to sea, the water was almost glassy calm. About twenty miles out, they sighted a small island, green and palm-fringed.

Joe gave a whoop of triumph. "Frank, I believe your hunch about a hideout north of Cabezona is paying off!"

"Where to now?" Tony asked. "Do we make a landing?"

"That's what we came for," Frank said grimly as he shaded his eyes to peer shoreward.

The tiny island was narrow and stringbean-shaped, with its long axis lying north and south. Tony cruised cautiously until he found an opening in the coral reef surrounding the islet. Then he steered towards the beach through the gentle breakers, and anchored in shallow water. The boys kicked off their sandshoes and waded ashore.

"I wonder if any of the gang is lurking around," Joe murmured when they reached the sandy beach, which sparkled bone-white in the sunshine. "Maybe we should have—"

He broke off, startled, as a horde of wild-eyed natives sprang from a dense thicket of greenery. Waving clubs and knives, they charged at the boys with blood-chilling yells!

"Run for it!" yelled Frank.

The boys plunged into the water and ploughed back to the boat. As Chet, in the rear, squirmed aboard, Frank revved the engine and steered out to a safe distance. Back near shore, the natives stood waist-deep in water, still yelling and shaking their weapons.

"Wow!" Joe gulped. "What started all that?"

"W-we did!" said Chet, trembling with fright. "We must have landed right in the middle of the gang's hideout. Those cannibals are standing guard for 'em!"

"Cannibals nothing!" said Tony. "I'll bet those are Carib Indians. Isn't that what they call the original inhabitants of these parts?"

"Call 'em anything you like," Chet replied. "They're still heap bad medicine!"

The stout boy was all for returning to San Juan. But the other three managed to persuade him that they should explore further.

With Frank at the helm, they cruised along the western shore of the island. Presently they came to a small cove, which formed a snug little natural harbour. Alongside a pier which jutted out into the water a red motorboat was moored. Near the shore lay a palatial white villa.

"Must be some millionaire's holiday home," Chet

marked. "But I wouldn't want to be that close to
ose natives!"

On higher ground behind the estate the boys
impsed an airstrip with a plane on it much like the
ardys' craft, except that it was silver in colour.

"Should we tie up and look round?" Chet asked.

"Not yet," said Frank. "Let's cruise a bit farther
st, and get the lay of the land."

Continuing along the coast, they circled the northern
p of the island. It was covered with pineapple fields,
ut there was no sign of workers or natives.

"Guess we may as well go back," Frank remarked.

He reversed course and steered back round the
land. As they neared the tiny harbour, a man waved
eerfully from the pier.

"Hi, there!" he shouted. "Come on in!"

Frank brought the boat to shore, and they tied up to
e dock on the opposite side from the red motorboat.
he man who had called to them was a stout and
ffable-looking person, wearing an immaculate white
it and puffing on a cigar.

"Glad to see you," he greeted the boys as they
imbed on to the pier. "We don't often have visitors.
urling Hamilton's my name," he added.

The boys shook hands and introduced themselves.
hey learned that Hamilton was a retired sportsman,
ho spent most of his time on the island estate.

"What brings you boys out here?" he queried.

"We're hunting for a gang of thieves," Chet blurted
efore Frank or Joe could stop him.

Hamilton appeared not to notice the awkward
lence that followed. "Well, I wish you luck." He

smiled. "Got quite a problem myself. Confounde
natives just south of here have made trouble for me eve
since I built my home on Calypso Island."

The Hardys and their friends tried not to look startle
at this remark. Casually Frank asked, "Did you sa
Calypso Island?"

Hamilton nodded. "That's what the natives call i
They're descendants of Carib Indians with some mixe
blood. They practise voodoo and worship a small fla
stone—*Skeleton Rock*."

· 17 ·

Voodoo Vengeance

HERE at last was a real clue! Frank and Joe guessed that probably the natives of Calypso Island were being used as a screen by the smugglers. So it was only natural that they should try to drive Durling Hamilton off the island.

"Have the natives been doing anything unusual lately?" Joe asked the sportsman. "I mean, have you noticed mysterious ceremonies?"

Hamilton puffed his cigar for a moment. "Well," he replied, "I did see a blue speedboat put in on the natives' side of the island yesterday."

"A blue boat!" Tony's eyes flashed excitedly.

"That's right," Hamilton went on. "Four men came ashore."

"Did you get a good look at them?" Frank asked eagerly.

"Yes. I watched them through binoculars. About all I can tell you, though, is that one was a tall, heavy-set fellow. They talked with the Indians for a while and then sailed off."

A tall, heavy-set fellow! The boys exchanged knowing glances. Could he have been Abdul?

Hamilton interrupted their thoughts by inviting the

boys up to his villa for lunch. A few minutes later th
group was seated in comfortable wicker chairs on th
terrace enjoying lemonade, pineapple salad, an(
sandwiches of cold roast beef.

Apart from his staff of white-jacketed Puerto Ricans
Hamilton appeared to live alone on the estate. "It'
nice to have company," he told his guests.

After lunch their host showed the boys his gam(
room, decorated with huge trophies of marlin, sailfish
and barracuda. Then he suggested a couple of fast set
of tennis which he refereed, on twin courts near th
airstrip. Afterwards, all of them cooled off with ;
refreshing swim in the gentle blue waters of the cove
By this time, it was late in the afternoon.

"You've given us a wonderful time, sir," Frank tol(
Hamilton when the boys had finished dressing. "Nov
we'd better start back to San Juan."

"Nonsense!" The sportsman paused to bite off th
tip of a fresh cigar. "As I told you, we don't have man·
visitors out here. Gets mighty lonesome. I want yo·
boys to stay and be my guests as long as you like."

Chet and Tony, though eager to extend their visit
left the decision to the Hardys. Frank and Joe wer
excited about the possibility of doing more exploring
But, to throw Hamilton off the scent, they delib
erately hesitated in accepting the invitation.

"At least stay overnight," Hamilton urged. "If yo·
get bored, you can go back tomorrow morning."

"Well, if you put it like that, Mr Hamilton"—Fran·
grinned—"I guess we'll accept your invitation."

"Fine, wonderful!" their portly host beamed. "I'·
cook part of the dinner myself. I'm quite a chef in m

pare time," he boasted. "I'm counting on some real appetites to do it justice!"

The dinner of rock lobster and red snapper proved to be delicious. Both Frank and Joe took only the snapper, which was broiled to juicy perfection. But Tony and Chet ate liberally of both dishes.

After dinner they strolled out on the terrace under the stars. Chet sank into a deep lounge chair and let his head loll back.

"O-oh," he groaned. "I must've eaten too much."

"Is that unusual?" Joe needled.

"No kidding," Chet replied. "My stomach feels like lead!"

Tony looked a bit unhappy too. "I don't feel so well myself," he confessed.

As the boys continued to feel uncomfortable, Durling Hamilton became concerned. "Just sit there and take it easy," he advised. "I'm sure it'll pass off. Too much excitement for one day, maybe—not good for the digestion!"

Meanwhile, Frank and Joe decided to do some sleuthing round the southern end of the island. Saying that they needed exercise, they excused themselves and wandered off along the smooth, sandy beach.

Darkness had fallen, and a full yellow moon was rising over the water. A cool trade wind wafted through the palm trees.

Suddenly Frank gripped his brother's arm. "Look! A campfire!" he pointed.

The flickering orange flames were visible through the dark foliage a short distance back from the beach.

"Come on!" Joe whispered. "Let's see what's up!"

Creeping closer, they pulled aside some branches and saw a group of natives squatting about the fire. The Indians, clad in ragged shirts and trousers, were jabbering excitedly.

"They're sure upset about something," Joe murmured.

"Hamilton said they practise voodoo," Frank whispered. "Maybe they're getting ready for some kind of ceremony."

As the boys listened they caught several words spoken in Spanish. "Sounds more like an argument," Joe noted.

Presently a skinny brown dog that was curled up near the campfire got to his feet and began to sniff the night air.

"Oh, oh!" gulped Joe in a low voice. "Let's hope he doesn't pick up our scent!"

Slowly the dog began to circle the camp, coming nearer and nearer to the boys' hiding place. All of a sudden he stiffened and broke into a volley of barks.

The natives stopped talking immediately and grabbed up heavy sticks. The Hardys flattened themselves in the underbrush. Should they lie still, or try to make a break?

The decision was made for them when the Indian strode towards the spot. Encouraged by his masters, the snarling cur charged into the thicket.

Instantly Frank and Joe sprang up and started to run. But before they had gone a dozen paces, the fleet-footed natives overtook them. Several grabbed the boys while others menaced them with clubs.

"Don't fight!" Frank called to his brother. "Maybe
we can convince them we're friends."

Trying to appear calm, the boys allowed themselves
to be dragged back to the campfire. One of the natives,
a youth about their own age, was able to speak a little
English.

"Me Fernando," he told them. "What you do here?
You come to spy for rich white man?"

"No," Frank replied. "We're just visitors here on the
island. We saw your campfire and wondered what was
going on, that's all."

As the boy translated, there was an angry babble
from the other natives. Fernando turned back to the
Hardys.

"They say you enemies—you work for Señor
Hamilton," he said accusingly. "Him bad man! Our
people live here on island always. This our home. Then
he come—try to drive us away!"

Frank and Joe denied this earnestly. Speaking in
simple words, they tried to convince the youth that they
wished to be friends and that Durling Hamilton had no
designs against the natives. But it was clear from the
Indians' scowling faces that the words were having no
effect.

Finally Joe decided to speak out bluntly. "Look, Fernando," he asked, "is it true that your people believe in
voodoo and worship something called Skeleton Rock?"

The effect of Joe's question was astounding. At the
mention of Skeleton Rock, the natives seemed to go
wild. Shouting and babbling in mixed Spanish-Indian
dialect, they seized the two boys and hurled them to the
ground!

Frank and Joe fought like wildcats but were soon tied hand and foot. Then the natives began to drag them down to the water's edge.

"They're going to throw us to the sharks!" Joe gasped to his brother.

"You two boys bad like Hamilton!" Fernando glared at them. "Now my people take revenge!"

The Hardys turned pale, their hearts hammering with fear as the Indians loaded them into a boat. Again and again, they pleaded to be released, speaking in both Spanish and English.

Finally their words seemed to take effect. There was a lot of babbling among the natives, then one spoke to Fernando.

He translated, "We let you go. But you must leave the island and never come back!"

"You have our promise," Frank assured him fervently. "We'll go tomorrow."

As soon as they were untied, the boys hurried on down the beach. Both were baffled by their close brush with death and its relation to Hamilton. Was he more deeply involved than the natives had indicated?

"And why did they get so excited just because I mentioned Skeleton Rock?" Joe puzzled.

Frank shook his head in bewilderment. "Search me unless the smuggling gang fooled them into thinking that any outsiders are dangerous. Or, maybe 'Skeleton Rock' is a sacred name."

As they neared Hamilton's villa, they saw a lighted cigar glowing in the dark on the front terrace.

"Have an interesting walk?" the sportsman greeted them.

"We sure did!" Frank said dryly.

A Puerto Rican servant escorted them to a guest room next to Chet and Tony's. Chet was moaning in distress when the Hardys went in to see him.

"Feeling any better, Chet?" Joe inquired sympathetically.

"Worse!" the plump boy replied. He was stretched out on the bed like a beached whale, in a pair of flowery pyjamas provided by their host.

Tony was not so ill as Chet, but he looked worried. As soon as the servant was out of earshot, he whispered to Frank and Joe:

"Listen! I went out on the dock for some fresh air and noticed that Hamilton's red boat looked awfully shiny in the moonlight. When I touched it, the red paint came off on my finger!"

The Hardys' eyes widened with interest. "Was it blue underneath?" Joe asked breathlessly.

"Before I had a chance to find out, I heard someone behind me and turned round. It was Hamilton!"

· 18 ·

A Weird Vision

"HAMILTON!" exclaimed Frank. "Do you think he wa
spying on you?"

Tony shrugged. "I'm not sure. But he was right ther
watching when I tested the paint."

The Hardys, having heard what the natives had sai
about Hamilton, were not surprised. This latest infor
mation definitely seemed to put their host unde
suspicion!

Joe urged that the boys confront Hamilton immedi
ately.

But Frank was more cautious. "Hamilton has
whole crew of servants. If they're part of the gang, the
could do plenty!"

"What's the difference?" Joe said stubbornly. "I
Hamilton is a member of the gang, we're in danger
anyway. Maybe he even slipped something into thos
lobsters Chet and Tony ate!"

Tony gasped. "You mean we've been poisoned?"

"Not deadly poison, but something he hoped woul
make all of us sick enough so that we couldn't do an
investigation and would have to go home."

Frank was still doubtful. "In that case, why did h
invite us to stay on the island?"

"So he could keep tabs on us until he had a chance to report to the gang," Joe suggested.

In the end, Frank agreed to put the question of speaking to Hamilton to a vote. Chet was feeling too sick to care one way or the other, but Tony sided with Joe. So the three boys went off to find Hamilton. But they agreed not to arouse the man's suspicions if they could avoid it.

The sportsman was still on the terrace, finishing his cigar.

"Is Chet feeling better?" he asked affably.

"Not much," Frank replied. "But I don't understand it. Lobster never seemed to bother him before."

Hamilton grinned. "I think your friend had too much to eat. Lobster's very rich."

Tony, changing the subject, told Durling Hamilton about his boat *Napoli II*, and of several exciting adventures he had had in her. Then he remarked casually, "But she needs a new paint job right now. What did you use on your motorboat, Mr Hamilton? I noticed before that it was freshly painted."

The sportsman smiled. "Not the whole boat. I had the bow touched up today because of rust spots on it. By the way, Tony, you seem to be feeling better now."

"Yes, thank you." Casually the boy added, "Lucky for me, though, that you came out to the dock that time. I felt a little woozy."

"I was afraid of that," Hamilton said, giving him an ingratiating smile. "As host here, it's my duty to look after my guests, isn't it?"

Hamilton seemed so frank that the boys found it hard

to remain suspicious. After chatting a few minutes longer, they said good night and returned to their rooms. Chet was asleep.

In spite of the cool trade winds, both Frank and Joe were unable to fall asleep. Their minds were overactive, and they were alert for any unusual happenings. About two o'clock they were roused from a deep sleep by a humming engine somewhere in the distance.

"It's a plane!" Joe whispered.

The boys rushed to the window. As the drone of the engine grew louder, they saw the craft swoop down as if for a landing on the airstrip. Then it pulled up abruptly and circled round. Its green starboard light began blinking.

"A message!" said Frank as the light spelled "Okay H."

"What does that mean?" Joe asked.

"It could be Hamilton or Hardy," Frank replied.

As they stood watching, the plane soared off and disappeared into the night. Thoroughly mystified, the two boys went back to bed, full of conjectures, mostly about their own safety. They had just fallen into a light slumber when a shriek from the next room made them sit bolt upright.

"Chet!" Frank said. "He must be worse!"

The Hardys dashed to the next room. Chet was quiet now, but trembling violently. He stood by a window, pointing.

Tony, sleepy-eyed, was already on his feet. " 'Smatter, Chet?" he asked.

"A g-g-ghost!" the boy quavered. "I just saw a ghost! O-o-o-oh, it was horrible!"

"A ghost?" Frank echoed blankly. "Good grief, what're you talking about, Chet?"

"It's true!" he insisted. "My stomach ache got so bad I couldn't sleep, so I got up. Then I looked out the window and I saw it—a huge Indian war chief, shining all over with a white glow! I'd say the thing's somewhere up at the north end of the island."

"If it was that far away, how could you see the thing?" asked Tony.

"Because he was so big, that's why! I'm telling you, he towered way up over the trees!" Just thinking about the fearsome sight seemed to turn Chet's face a more sickly hue than ever.

"Chet's really ill," said Joe. "He's delirious!"

"I'm not delirious!" Chet insisted frantically. "Golly, can't you be—"

"Okay, okay, we believe you," Frank said soothingly. "But please go back to sleep and try to get some rest." After a while Chet calmed down and the Hardys returned to their room.

Early the next morning Frank and Joe leaped out of bed.

"Let's get down to the dock and take a peek at that boat!" said Frank.

Without waiting for breakfast, the boys dashed out of the villa and hurried down to the pier. They ran their fingers over the red motorboat. The paint seemed perfectly dry except for a few tacky brush marks near the bow.

"I guess Hamilton was telling the truth," said Frank. "This clears him."

"Thanks!" said a chuckling voice.

Whirling in surprise, the boys saw their host watching them from the inward end of the pier. He strolled out to join them, his ruddy face enveloped in a friendly smile.

"Don't think I'm spying, now," he said jovially, "but I couldn't help notice you test that paint. You're real detectives, yes sir! But you can trust old Durling Hamilton!"

Somewhat embarrassed, the Hardys asked about the plane they had seen the previous night.

"Oh, that!" Hamilton laughed heartily. "That was a friend of mine—fellow sportsman, you might say—named Steve Henry. He was just passing over on his way from Miami to Puerto Rico, so he stopped off to say hello. Always gives me that old blinker signal whenever he goes by this way."

Mentally, Frank and Joe had to admit that Hamilton's answer seemed reasonable. If his friend's name was Henry, that would explain the initial H at the end of the message.

Excusing themselves, the Hardys went back to the house to see how Chet and Tony were feeling. Tony was much better, but, to their dismay, they found Chet so weak he could hardly move.

"He's really in bad shape," Tony whispered.

Their stout chum lay almost motionless on the bed, moaning weakly from time to time.

"We'd better get a doctor, pronto!" Frank decided. "You stay here with Chet, Tony."

He and Joe hurried downstairs and reported their friend's condition to Hamilton. "We want a doctor right away," Joe urged.

Luckily the estate owner had a radio-telephone connection to San Juan. He put through a call to the mainland immediately, then turned to the boys.

"There's a break!" he announced. "This doctor friend of mine I just called is taking the day off. He's fishing in his favourite spot about five miles from here. With luck, you can get back here in no time!"

He suggested the boys take his red motorboat, which was faster than their own. Frank and Joe gladly accepted and he sent word to have it fuelled and readied for the trip.

"Watch out for sharks!" Hamilton warned when the Hardys prepared to cast off. "These waters are infested with the brutes!"

Beyond the reef, the sea turned choppy as a spanking breeze whipped the water into white-caps. Frank and Joe headed south towards Puerto Rico, following their host's directions.

Several times they saw the fins of sharks knifing past. When their craft reached the fishing spot Hamilton had described, the doctor's boat was nowhere in sight.

Joe scanned the horizon anxiously. "Do you suppose Hamilton lied to us?" he muttered.

"Just what I was wondering," Frank replied. Suddenly he gave a cry of alarm. "Joe! The boat's leaking!"

A steady stream of water was gushing in from the motor compartment!

Hastily the boys whipped off their shirts and Joe crawled into the compartment with them to plug the leak. When he emerged a moment later, half-soaked and oil-smeared, his face was taut.

"There's a big round hole in the hull!" he reported.

"Looks as if it was partly cut out with a saw, and sea pressure did the rest!"

"Hamilton!" gasped Frank.

"Sure looks that way. No wonder he was so eager to have us take this boat!"

There was no time to debate the matter further. They took off their jeans and stuffed them in the hole. But already there was too much water in the boat for them to do any good. To make matters worse, the engine suddenly stopped.

"Maybe there's a pump in the locker," Frank suggested hopefully. He opened the seat to look, then gave a startled cry as he dragged out a red, green, and white pennant.

It was the foreign flag, with a black skeleton added in the lower right-hand corner!

"Just like the one we found in Hugo's trailer!" exclaimed Joe. "Say, what *is* Hamilton's tie-up with that fortune teller?"

Frank did not reply. The plugs in the hull suddenly gave way and more water gushed into the boat. Desperately the boys groped in the locker. There were three life jackets, but no pump.

Just then the drone of a plane drew their attention. Waving wildly, they tried to attract the pilot. Once he dipped and the boys were sure he saw them. But the silver-coloured plane went on.

"I'll bet that was Hamilton!" said Frank, clenching his teeth grimly.

"Yes," Joe stormed helplessly. "Everything those natives said about him was right! And he came out here to watch us battle the sharks!"

· 19 ·

Skeleton Rock

"AT LEAST we have knives. That'll be some protection against the sharks," Joe said grimly. "If any of them want a bite out of me they'll have to fight for it!"

"Right!" Frank pulled out two of the life jackets and handed one to Joe.

They put them on. Then, arming themselves with their pocketknives, the two boys waited tensely. By this time, the water in the boat was up to their knees.

The boys had been so busy watching the water that they had not noticed a plane approaching the area.

"Hamilton again, I suppose," Frank said angrily as he looked up.

Suddenly Joe gave a happy shout. "It's *our* plane!"

The boys hardly dared believe their eyes.

"Do you suppose Dad and Jack are aboard?" Joe asked hopefully. "And they've come to rescue us?"

Frank and Joe waved their arms frantically, yelling as loudly as they could. The plane circled and swooped in low. Jack Wayne was at the controls.

"Yippee!" shouted Joe.

The pilot waved back to the boys reassuringly. Mr Hardy was not in the plane. A moment later the cabin door opened and an inflated life raft tumbled down towards the water.

It landed with a splash several yards away from the boat, but Frank was overboard in a moment to swim to it. He climbed inside, then picked up Joe.

As soon as the boys were safely afloat, Jack dipped his wings, then began to circle the area.

"Too bad he couldn't haul us into the plane," Joe remarked.

A half hour of anxious waiting followed. Sharks bobbed up repeatedly, close to the raft. Finally a government patrol boat appeared and Jack flew off as soon as the Hardys were helped to the deck of the rescue craft.

"Lucky you're not minus a few toes," declared the captain with grim humour.

"How'd you find us?" Joe asked.

"Jack Wayne radioed an SOS," the captain replied. "Better go below, fellows, and get some hot soup. We'll have you back at San Juan before you dry off!"

Jack was waiting to greet them there at the dock. "Man, am I glad to see you two!" he exclaimed.

"Not half as glad as we were to see *you!*" Joe quipped as they shook hands. "Did you know it was Frank and me stranded on the water?"

"No. I saw that the boat was not moving and decided to take a closer look. What happened?"

Frank described their visit to Calypso Island and his suspicions about Hamilton. Jack flushed with anger. "The skunk!" he cried out. But a moment later he said, "I just had another thought. Maybe one of those natives who hates Hamilton put the hole in his boat."

"That's right," Joe agreed. "It seems as if every time we suspect that man there's a sound reason to excuse him."

But Frank was not so charitable. "I'm sure Hamilton was in that first plane which wouldn't give us any help. Well, Jack, what's the news from Dad? Where is he now?"

Jack's face became grave. "I'm worried about him," he replied. "After we took off from here, I flew your father to Centro, Tropicale. He said that if he didn't show up at the airport by twelve o'clock last night, I should go get you boys and try to find him. Well, he didn't show up!"

The news sent a shock of alarm through the boys. Centro was the spot where they had tangled in the gunfight between police and rebels! Could the gang have sought revenge on their father?

"We ought to fly to Tropicale as soon as possible," Joe urged.

"And we must get help to Chet," Frank reminded him. "Let's stop at a doctor's on the way to the airport and talk to him."

A taxi driver they consulted took them to the office of Dr Roberto Cortez, just a few yards from the waterfront. After hearing their story, the doctor reassured the boys.

"From the symptoms you describe, I am sure that your friend will be no worse. If he had been given a harsh poison, he would have been in great pain last evening. But I'll write you a prescription which should ease the young man's difficulties."

Greatly relieved, the boys thanked Dr Cortez and

hurried off to the nearest chemist's. While waiting for the prescription to be filled, they discussed what to do.

"We can fly to Calypso Island, give Chet the medicine, and make arrangements for the hired boat to be returned to its owner. Then all of us can go on to Tropicale," Frank suggested.

"Good idea," Joe agreed.

When they reached the airport, Jack Wayne refuelled the Hardy plane for take-off. But as he started to warm up the engine, it gave a sputter and died. The pilot could not restart it.

Wearily Jack climbed out and went to work on the defective engine. "Plugs aren't firing," he announced after a brief inspection.

Impatient and worried, the Hardys stood by while Jack traced the trouble to a faulty magneto. Then came another long delay while he went off to hunt for a replacement.

It was late afternoon before the plane was finally ready for take-off. To the Hardys' relief, the engine purred smoothly as they soared off towards Calypso Island.

"What about Hamilton?" Joe asked Frank. "You suppose he'll give us any trouble?"

Frank shrugged. "No telling. I have a feeling that man is very slick."

Both boys took brief turns at the controls, and Joe brought the plane down on Hamilton's airstrip for a perfect landing.

The estate owner came out to greet them. "Welcome back!" He smiled. "I see you found a faster method for the return trip."

"We had to," Frank said curtly, introducing Jack. "Your boat sank."

"What!" Hamilton appeared genuinely shocked when the boys told him about the hole in the speedboat's hull.

"Sabotage!" he stormed. "Those confounded Carib Indians must have done it!"

For several minutes he ranted angrily against the natives. The sportsman seemed so genuinely upset that Joe glanced at Frank as if to say, "Maybe Hamilton is innocent after all."

"How's Chet?" Frank asked, interrupting the sportsman. "We brought him some medicine."

"I guess he won't need it," Hamilton replied with a cheery grin. "In fact, he and Tony were feeling so much better, they decided to go off and do a little spying on the Indians."

"Why?" Frank asked.

"Professional jealousy, I'd guess." Hamilton chuckled. "Your chubby friend figured the two of them might solve a mystery about the natives before you boys got back. Well, let's go up to the house and get some supper."

The Hardys were puzzled and uncertain what to do. Could they trust the estate owner's story and fly on to Tropicale? But, talking it over privately at the villa, they decided it was too risky to leave until they knew for certain that their friends were safe.

After a tasty supper, Frank asked, "Mr Hamilton, don't you think Chet and Tony should be back by this time?"

"Perhaps so, but I shouldn't worry about them."

Frank and Joe could not accept Hamilton's suggestion. They had to find out where their friends were. Excusing themselves, they set out with Jack Wayne for the southern end of the island.

They made a point of avoiding the open beach as they pushed their way through the palm groves and underbrush. It was dark now, but the rising moon shed enough light for them to see where they were going.

Soon the boys sighted the glimmering windows of a cluster of native shacks. Natives were milling about outside, jabbering excitedly.

"Something's up," Jack observed. "I wonder if Chet and Tony are being held prisoner."

As the pilot started forward, Frank grabbed his arm to stop him. "Joe and I have had one set-to with these Indians," he whispered. "Let's keep out of sight. We promised them we'd leave the island for good today."

Staying in the shadows, the three circled the village. Suddenly Joe caught sight of Fernando. By hissing, he managed to attract the youth's attention.

"Why have you come back?" Fernando exclaimed worriedly as he joined them. "You are in terrible danger here if my people find you!"

"We'll go quickly if you'll help us," Frank promised. "We only came back to find our two friends."

"Your two friends?" The boy looked puzzled.

Frank and Joe explained that their friends had come to call on the Indians. Fernando denied that he or his people had seen them.

The Hardys had fresh cause for worry! Where *were* Chet and Tony? Was Hamilton making up the story of their whereabouts?

Before leaving, Joe asked one more question. "Tell me, Fernando, why did your people get so angry when I asked about Skeleton Rock?"

The young Carib shuddered. "It is a terrible place, *amigo!* It is at the other end of the island, but do not go there! Sometimes at night the ghost of an old cacique rises up to devour men's souls!"

The words were hardly out of Fernando's mouth when he turned pale with fright. "Look! Look!" he quavered, pointing northwards. "He is there now!"

As the others turned, a fantastic sight met their eyes. Looming above the distant treetops was the huge figure of an ancient Carib chieftain. The spectre glowed with a weird white radiance.

"Jumping cacti!" gasped Jack Wayne.

"So that's what Chet saw last night!" added Joe. "No wonder he couldn't sleep!"

The whole village seethed with turmoil as the natives wailed and quaked in alarm.

"What do you make of it?" Jack asked.

"I believe that ghost is a plant by the gang to keep these natives in subjection," Frank replied.

"Yes," Joe agreed, "and it might have been put into action right now to scare *us* away."

"I feel sure," said Frank, "that Hamilton is involved in this and in Chet and Tony's disappearance. Come on! I think we'd better radio a message for help from our plane to the authorities in Puerto Rico."

As they reached the airstrip, the three crept towards the plane under cover of darkness. Joe warmed up the radio and started sending a message to San Juan. Finally the harbour police replied.

"Calling from Calypso Island!" Joe spoke urgently into the mike. "This is an emergency. Two boys—"

Joe got no further. A gunshot cracked in the distance. Then two more rang out as a horde of armed men rushed towards the airstrip from the villa. Though still out of effective range, they were shooting wildly at the plane. One bullet pinged off a rock near the craft.

"Look, Hamilton's leading them!" yelled Frank, recognizing the man at the head of the gang. "Get going, Jack!"

The pilot grimly went to work. The starter whined, but nothing else happened.

"Mixture control is jammed!" he groaned. Jumping up, he dashed aft for the tool kit.

Frank grabbed the controls and managed to free the mixture control before Jack returned. With a roar, the engine thundered into action!

As the plane taxied down the strip, another volley of shots ripped the night air. A moment later they were aloft and gaining altitude.

"Wow!" Joe relaxed weakly in his seat and wiped the perspiration from his forehead. "If the police heard the shooting, they ought to get here pronto!" Nevertheless, he continued to send out a call for help.

Soaring over the northern end of the island, Frank looked for the cacique's ghost, but the figure had disappeared.

A moment later Joe pointed down towards the beach. "Look!" he exclaimed. "There's Skeleton Rock!"

Below, in the moonlight, a curious formation was visible in the coral reef. A portion of the rocky shore line protruded above the water in the shape of a crude skeleton. Even the arms and legs were clearly defined.

"Weird!" said Jack. "Enough to make a fellow feel creepy. Now what do we do?"

"What Beppo tells you to, *amigos!*" came a sneering voice from the rear of the cabin.

The Hardys and Jack whirled in dismay. A blond figure had just emerged from the luggage compartment, clutching a pistol. It was the youth who resembled Joe!

"Turn back and land on Calypso!" he ordered.

· 20 ·

The Ghost's Secret

As FRANK hesitated, the blond youth came a step closer. His finger curled menacingly around the trigger of his gun.

"Do as I say," he snapped, "or you'll be sorry!"

Jack, who was occupying a rear seat, made a lunge for Beppo's weapon—but not in time. Swinging his heavy automatic, the gunman caught Jack on the side of the head with a vicious blow. Jack groaned and slumped unconscious!

Joe started towards Jack, but Beppo motioned him to sit beside Frank.

"Now turn this plane round," the gunman ordered Frank, "before you two get the same!"

Frank suddenly realized he was now on his own, with a gun at his back and no flight instructor to guide him. Although both the boys had flown before, neither of them had ever handled a plane of this size without Jack Wayne's guidance.

As they winged back towards Hamilton's villa, a daring plan occurred to the young pilot. He nudged Joe, to alert him that he would need help.

Suddenly Frank shoved the wheel forward! The plunging dive threw the gunman off-balance. As he lurched backwards, Joe grabbed the gun.

"Don't move!" barked Joe.

When the craft levelled off, Frank set the automatic pilot. Joe pulled some rope from a locker, and in moments the two boys had the gunman tightly bound.

"No wonder this guy looks like me, Frank. His features have been changed with make-up!"

Joe now came forward and Frank whispered, "This time I'm going to imitate our prisoner."

As they neared the landing field, Frank turned up the two-way radio, "Calling Hamilton!" Frank rasped, disguising his voice to sound like that of the prisoner. "All okay."

The receiver crackled in reply. "Good work, Beppo! Now we have the whole Hardy gang at Skeleton Rock. We can strike at once!"

The brother were stunned. So the smugglers had their father—and also Chet and Tony!

Frank gripped the controls, his brain working at top speed. How could they free Mr Hardy and their friends? Stalling for time to find an answer to the dilemma, he swooped low over the field, then banked and circled.

Again the radio crackled. "Don't fool around, Beppo! Hurry up and land them!"

"Now what?" gasped Joe in a low voice.

Uncertain of his next move, Frank climbed for altitude and circled once more. The engine began to putter, and with a final cough, died. Then the plane began bucking and plunging as it suddenly ran into severe turbulence.

Wildly Frank worked with the controls. What to do now? If they landed on the strip, they would both be captured. Hoping against hope that they would not lose altitude too rapidly, Frank glided for the northern end of the island.

"Maybe we can make the beach!" Joe cried.

With luck they could, Frank thought, as he eased the wheel forward. Both boys froze as the plane nosed downwards in a normal glide.

At the tip of the island, a broad strip of wet sand lay exposed by the low tide. With a great jolt the plane hit the beach, ploughed forward, and upended as its nose wheel gouged into the sand and collapsed. The craft was only a few yards from Skeleton Rock!

"Frank, you're a whiz!" Joe said shakily.

Frank smiled wanly, then said, "I hope the landing didn't make Jack worse."

At once they gently lifted the pilot's limp body out on to the beach. There was an ugly bruise on Jack's right temple. Frank chafed his wrists and bathed his face with water. Jack stirred slightly.

"How is he?" Joe asked anxiously.

"Breathing okay. He should revive completely in a little while."

A sudden cry from his brother made Frank snap bolt upright. "Look!" Joe gasped.

From a nearby pit a huge phosphorescent figure was emerging. It was the Indian chieftain's ghost, glowing weirdly in the moonlight!

"It's some kind of plastic balloon covered with phosphorescent paint!" Frank exclaimed. "What a stunt for scaring natives!"

"Well, that gang won't do it any longer!" Joe declared. Taking out his pocketknife, he darted forward and ripped the bag wide open.

There was a rush of escaping air. With a weak, moaning sound, the ghost balloon collapsed sideways in a brightly shining heap. As Frank watched it sink beside the pit, he cried out excitedly, "Joe! There's a trap door in that pit! I'll bet there's something else down there besides the balloon and gas machine."

"Loot, you mean?"

"Perhaps."

Together, the boys raised the door. A flight of stone steps led downwards into the coral rock.

Frank flicked on his pocket torch, and the boys descended cautiously. At the foot of the stairway, the passage opened into an underground room.

Three familiar voices cried out, "Frank! Joe!"

The Hardys stared in astonishment. Before them, trussed up, were Mr Hardy, Chet and Tony!

"Thank goodness you came! We must get out of here before those killers seal us up for good!"

Quickly Frank and Joe untied them, telling of their own narrow escape. The group rushed up the stone steps. They had just reached the beach when Hamilton and his attackers swarmed into view through the shrubbery.

"We're outnumbered three to one!" Tony cried in dismay.

Mr Hardy suggested that if they could subdue Hamilton, the suspected leader, perhaps the others would give up. As the smugglers closed in on them, he manoeuvred his way towards Hamilton, who had stepped to the side.

Hamilton was ready. He was about to strike the private detective with a heavy stone, when Chet came

to the rescue. Throwing his voice, he yelled, "Loo
behind you, Hamilton!"

The gang leader whirled in surprise, expecting a
attack. Fenton Hardy acted instantly. He delivered
punch that knocked Hamilton backwards and sent h
weapon flying through the air.

Meanwhile, the four boys had gone into actior
Blows were exchanged right and left as they flayed int
the mobsters.

"Keep it up!" Tony shouted excitedly.

But the tide of battle was turning in favour of th
gang. Outnumbered, Mr Hardy and the boys wer
being battered into defeat.

Then, just as the end seemed near, the fighters hear
wild war whoops above the din. Through the darknes
swooped a mob of Carib Indians! Fernando was wit
them.

"Fernando! Help us—the Hardys!" Joe shouted
"We are fighting your *real* enemies!"

The natives needed no urging. With clubs and sticks
they beat Hamilton's followers into howling panic.

When the battle was over, Frank rushed up t
Fernando. "Thanks! *Muchas gracias*, Fernando!" h
panted. "You sure saved the day!"

Among the captives the boys spotted Abdul an
Hugo, and pointed them out to their father. Then the
plied Mr Hardy with questions as to what had hap
pened to him in Tropicale.

The detective smiled. "Now the story can be told.
was working on a case involving subversives in th
United States friendly to a gang of rebels in Tropical
who hoped to take over the government. Those in ou

country have been rounded up with the exception of a few, like Abdul and Hugo, who escaped down here.

"Unfortunately, in uncovering a hideout in Tropicale, I was captured. Two men flew me here last night," he explained, "but apparently something went wrong. The plane couldn't land."

Joe snapped his fingers. "No wonder! Frank and I showed up here and Hamilton didn't want us to see you. Matter of fact, Frank and I read the plane's signal—'Okay H.' That must have been to let Hamilton know they'd captured you!"

The detective nodded. "The men finally brought me over this morning. I guess you two had left by that time."

"That's right," said Chet. "Then they tied Tony and me up and brought us to the dungeon. They planned to kill all of us and blame it on the Caribs. I'll say one thing, though," he added, chuckling. "Made me so mad I forgot all about my stomach ache!"

At that moment powerful searchlights began to sweep the island.

"Patrol ships!" Joe exclaimed. "Must be the police arriving from San Juan!"

Soon a boatload of armed policemen disembarked on to the beach. After Mr Hardy had given a brief account of the affair, the officers escorted the prisoners, including Beppo, back to Hamilton's villa. By this time, Jack Wayne had revived and was assisted there by the boys.

At the house Captain Valdez of the San Juan police held an official hearing. Mr Hardy cleared up the mystery.

"It was not until today that I learned who was masterminding a diabolical plot to overthrow the government of Tropicale. This man Hamilton is the one," the detective explained. "He organized an air-freight theft ring to seize various articles useful to his cause. Among these were isotopes to build an atomic weapon. Once completed, this would have given him and his gang absolute power over Tropicale. On the side, the men smuggled diamonds in dolls' or dummies' heads to help finance their crazy venture."

"It wasn't so crazy!" snarled the handcuffed Hamilton. "We might have pulled it off if that important Hugo dummy hadn't been sent to the very town where the Hardys live. Those nosy detectives and their pals upset our plans!"

"Tony and me?" Chet's eyes widened and his face glowed with pride.

"Yes, indeed," Captain Valdez praised them. "You all helped preserve peace in the Caribbean!"

"But how does the stolen drug, Variotrycin, come into the picture?" Frank asked his father. "And what about the brief case we found in the public locker in Eastern City? It was filled with the drug! In fact, after the man, who posed as Shanley, snatched it from us, we never saw him or the brief case again."

"The gang thought that stealing and selling the new drug would supplement their income in addition to the diamonds," Mr Hardy explained. "However, not enough of it was being manufactured to make it profitable. After the man impersonating Shanley snatched the brief case from you boys, he suddenly got greedy. He was arrested in New York City trying to sell the stuff."

Numerous other facts were brought out. "Skeleton Rock" was the gang's identification, and they had used the same device on their revolutionary pirate flag. The pineapple tattoos helped the members recognize one another.

"So that's why the cook at *El Calypso Caliente* got so upset when he spotted my tattoo!" said Joe. "He thought for a moment I was Beppo."

Mr Hardy nodded. "The restaurant was a regular meeting place for the gang."

Abdul, Hugo and many of Hamilton's island retainers now talked freely in the hope of getting light sentences. They revealed that a new red motorboat had been switched overnight for the blue one which Hamilton had tried to disguise with a fresh coat of paint. They also admitted that some mild poison had been put in the lobsters served at dinner.

"Too bad we didn't make the dose twice as strong," growled Hamilton.

The mysterious "doctor friend" was just a ruse to send Frank and Joe to their doom. Abdul also admitted that he lived in the old pink stucco house in San Juan, and that the basket device had been used to pick up loot and messages.

"How about the Hugo dummy?" Frank asked his father. "Was the Mexican manufacturer involved?"

"No," his father replied. "Hamilton's gang put the purple turbans on the dummies, inserted the glass eyes, and acted as distributors. Radley discovered this and notified me shortly after I saw you boys last."

Frank snapped his fingers. "I get it now! As distributors, Hamilton and his gang substituted the old-fashioned glass eyes for the original plastic ones in the Hugos and concealed the contraband and messages inside."

"The changed instruction sheet, too!" Joe chimed in.

"Right!" Mr Hardy said. "That code in Spanish was an extra precaution!" The detective added that the Hugos were shipped to bona fide customers in the United States, such as Mr Bivven in Bayport. "Gang members were on hand," he said, "to purchase the purple-turbanned Hugos immediately and get the diamonds."

"Then why," Chet burst in, "did those hoodlums snatch the red-turbanned dummy at Mr Bivven's place?"

Hearing this, Hamilton snapped, "Bivven, the old goat, fouled up the whole plan. He said that was his only Hugo, so my men figured I must have made a mistake in the colour of the turban."

At this point, a seaman from one of the patrol boats brought a radio message to Mr Hardy. It was a report from the Tropicale police, saying they had rounded up the remaining gang members from information relayed by Fenton Hardy before he was captured.

"Well, boys, I guess we can now get a good night's sleep!" The detective sighed.

"Believe me, you have earned it, señores!" Captain Valdez congratulated them. "I give you permission to use the villa. Mr Hamilton won't need it tonight!"

In a few days the Hardys' damaged plane was repaired, and they took off for San Juan. Jack Wayne urged Frank and Joe to demonstrate their flying skill to their father.

After watching them, the detective grinned. "Looks as if I have a couple of budding air aces in the family!"

His grin grew wider as Joe made a beautiful landing. A crowd of officials and newsmen were waiting on the field to greet the passengers.

An envoy of the Tropicale Government stepped forward and pinned a medal on the private investigator. "In token of your distinguished efforts for the cause of peace and justice!" He beamed.

"Thank you," Mr Hardy said, smiling, "but these boys here deserve it more than I do!"

"We know the part your sons played," said an airline official. "As a reward, my company is presenting them with this DME—Distance Measuring Equipment unit for the Hardys' private plane!"

"And for their friend Tony," said the Tropicale official, "we have a special boat trip in Caribbean waters."

With a broad smile Tony accepted, unaware of the exciting role he would play in helping the Hardy Boys solve many more mysteries in the future.

One more gift was presented and unwrapped—a whole family of ventriloquist dummies for Chet!

"Without diamonds, however," the official said, laughing.

Excitedly Chet seized one of the dummies and put on an impromptu act.

"Who cares about diamonds!" the largest one squawked. "When do we eat?"

Here are some of the most recent titles in our excitin
fiction series:

☐ Danger: Due North *J. J. Fortune* £1.75
☐ The Chalet School Triplets
  Elinor M. Brent-Dyer £1.75
☐ Legion of the Dead *J. H. Brennan* £1.95
☐ The Bluebeard Room *Carolyn Keene* £1.75
☐ The Swamp Monster *Franklin W. Dixon* £1.75
☐ The Mystery of the Smashing Glass
  Marc Brandel £1.75
☐ Horse of Fire *Patricia Leitch* £1.75
☐ Cry of a Seagull *Monica Dickens* £1.75

Armadas are available in bookshops and newsagents, but ca
also be ordered by post.

HOW TO ORDER
ARMADA BOOKS, Cash Sales Dept., GPO Box 29
Douglas, Isle of Man, British Isles. Please send purchas
price plus 15p per book (maximum postal charge £3.00)
Customers outside the UK also send purchase price plus 15
per book. Cheque, postal or money order – no currency.

NAME (Block letters) _____

ADDRESS_____

_____

_____